Jimmy Threepwood and the Veil of Darkness

By
Rich Pitman

Edited by Jessica Flaherty

Published by
Crimson Cloak Publishing

ISBN 13: 978-1-68160-426-8
ISBN 10: 1-68160-426-4

Publisher's Publication in Data:
Pitman, Rich
Jimmy Threepwood and the Veil of Darkness
1.Juvenile Fiction 2. Dark Fantasy 3. Growing up 4. Mystery
5. Demons

To Osho

Thank you
for uncovering
the Veil of Darkness

For Lottie Christine Pitman, the light in my life.

Prologue

Screams echoed off the cavern walls as a dark, cloaked creature glided over the damp floor; slowly, silently. What sounded like a thousand souls perishing by fire, rattled over the rocky surface as the creature - otherwise known as the Gatekeeper - stopped in the centre of a large, open space, where stood a giant mirror. Gazing into the reflection, he admired his handiwork; the souls he'd dragged, screaming from the mortal world into an eternity of suffering and pain, swirled and swirled behind the glass. Returning his attention to the grand mirror, he touched the bony remains of his finger to the glassy surface, liquefying it and opening a view into the world of man. The Gatekeeper surveyed the poorly populated Close of Mountbatten with hungry eyes and an evil laugh.

"Soon, Jimmy Threepwood, it will be your eleventh birthday. So starts the series of events which will bring an end to this mortal world, giving me an unlimited supply of souls to do my bidding!" The hellish creature gave a long, vile, thunderous laugh, which resonated throughout the unearthly prison.

Chapter 1

*H*ow *boring*, thought Jimmy Damien Threepwood as his breath fogged up the window that he gazed longingly out of. Jimmy was a small lad of ten years, although quite rotund for his size. He had a mop of ginger hair and a beaming smile, which had got him out of trouble on a number of occasions.

Looking around his small and lifeless bedroom he saw his wardrobe and chest of drawers sitting in the shadowy corner, housing only school uniform, a few of his clothes, cobwebs and spiders. For a boy of his age there was one thing clearly missing ... toys. Jimmy's mother didn't believe in toys or allow him any type of games; not even a computer. Instead, every Sunday, he was given a list of chores which often included washing the family car, cleaning his room, and generally doing the housework his mother refused to do. Did this really matter to him? Not really, he didn't know any better.

Jimmy continued to stare out of the window, longing to go outside and play football with his friends who lived on the council estate. Staring off to the right, in the direction of the estate, he was mesmerised by the nasty looking thick black clouds, which hung suspiciously in the air. Regular crackles of lightning snapped through the sky and each time they did so an uneasy feeling began growing in his stomach, especially as these black clouds were always in the same place every day, hanging high above the council estate projecting a sinister shadow on the ground below.

Feeling restless, he grabbed his sky-blue and white jumper from his bedside cabinet, pulled on his trainers and ran downstairs to see if his mother would let him go outside. Walking into the living room Jimmy was met with the usual foul smell of feet mixed with greasy food. There, slumped in an armchair, was his oversized slimy mother. She had a large sized fried chicken bucket resting on her stomach and a coke of the same size on the arm of her chair. Stains of the sticky liquid tainted the front of her grey vest top.

Engrossed in a daytime chat show, she didn't even notice him standing there.

"Mum, can I go out to play football?"

… Silence.

"Mum, can I ..."

Marjorie Threepwood turned her head, slowly peeling it away from the back of the armchair and scrunched her face into a disapproving look.

"I don't know. I don't care what you do! Go and see your father; can't you see I'm busy!" she said through gritted teeth, shooing him away and turning back to face the TV.

Solemnly lowering his gaze to the floor, suppressing sadness and tears, he shuffled slowly out to the garden to find his father.

As he reached the kitchen, the back door swung open and in walked a short, skinny man wearing round glasses clearly too big for his face and held in place by his long pointy nose.

Bill Threepwood ran his hand through his slicked back greying black hair.

"Arrhhh Jimmy, I was coming to find you. Why aren't you out playing football in the Close?"

"Dad, it's boring in the Close. It's too small. I want to go over the road on the grass to play football."

"Why don't you play in your room? Didn't I get you that toy you wanted the other day? Where's that gone ...?"

"... *Jimmy, is that you? What's taking you so long? I'm starving!*" a voice demanded from the living room.

The vision was so real he could almost touch it as he remembered walking into the living room two days earlier and handing his mother the chicken burger she had made him go out and collect.

"Puurrgh, what's this? It's freezing cold. You dawdled back again didn't you, DIDN'T YOU!? Right, that's it! Where's that stupid toy you wanted!?" his mother screamed, grabbing it from the mantelpiece. "I'm keeping this for one week; next time you won't dawdle will you? Out! Go to your room."

Jimmy remembered his lower lip quivering in response. "But, it wasn't my fault, it's what they gave me ..."

"I've heard enough. Go quickly, my programme's starting," his mother said as she grabbed the TV remote and turned away, slumping back into her chair.

Jimmy sat in his room on his own for hours. He had found a few old, plastic soldiers, most of which were snapped or broken as though they had been trodden on. He tried his best to use his imagination, to make up a game, but he could only think about his friends in school always talking about their new games and toys. Jimmy had to either pretend or keep his head down so he didn't get asked ...

"Mum took it away because I, urm, I was naughty," he mumbled dejectedly.

"Never mind, Jimmy. Look, go and play in your room or just outside, and I'll speak to your mother."

Shaking his head, Jimmy knew this wasn't going to end well. This happened every week, and every week he was forgotten about. He went back to his solemn, empty little grey room, lay down on his bed and wished with all of his might that things would change.

His head felt light as a feather and he could feel himself slowly, gently drifting off into a daydream. Suddenly he was jolted awake, nearly falling out of his bed, by the demonic reverberation of a thousand whips crackling through the sky. His heart was pounding and he was struggling to catch his breath as he forced his eyes open. He felt disorientated; he was no longer in his bedroom. Frantically looking down, he saw he was standing on hard, bone dry ground with cracks streaming off in all directions. The pungent smell of singed clothing and ozone oozed through his nostrils, making his senses tingle. Cracks of thunder made him jump and snap his neck upwards to see blood red and purple clouds gazing down at this young intruder. Burnt, ashen black trees caught his eye. He stared in disbelief. Petrified he looked around, searching for any means of escape ... and then he saw them.

In the near distance were vast numbers of lifeless bodies strewn across the scorched earth. Rushing to the closest person to see if he could help, Jimmy grabbed the shoulders and pulled the body over, gasping at what he saw. There was no face; no physical injury that he could see, just a vast void of emptiness where a face should have been. The body was wearing a black cloak with soft purple lining that had some form of animal emblem stitched into the breast pocket. The cloak was severely burnt. Brushing the soot away Jimmy was able to make out the head of an embroidered golden owl. Something made him reach into the open pocket of the cloak;

trembling and closing his eyes, his nervous fingertips touched a silky soft texture. He was just about to examine his find when, from behind him, came a roaring sound that seemed to shake the very ground and surrounding mountains.

Instinctively, Jimmy ducked, looking over his right shoulder to see what was happening. There in the distance two monstrous figures clashed blades again, sending a vibration through the air that made him stagger as it flicked past his tuft of hair. The figures were too far away to make out any real detail, but one was humongous with fiery red skin, a black cape thrashing in the wind and his hand raising a giant axe above his head. Jimmy couldn't turn to look at the other male; this humongous red warrior transfixed him. The ground quivered again as the hulky beast struck the final blow sending the second warrior hurtling through the air and crashing into a mighty oak.

Roaring in victory, the beast turned to see Jimmy kneeling next to one of his victims. In a flash it bounded towards him at immense speed, its strides eating up the distance. Fear flooded Jimmy's body, and he didn't know whether to run or fight.

He turned to run but found his legs wouldn't move. In sheer panic he tried again, but nothing. The warrior was getting closer and closer.

"Arrgh!"

Jimmy closed his eyes and woke up in his own bed in a pool of sweat. He took a long deep breath. His dream had felt so real. The burnt smell was still on his pyjama top, the black soot on his fingers … but he was safe.

He wiped the sweat away. Lying there for a short while trying to recover, he heard his mother and father talking downstairs. Glancing at the clock, he saw it was late. He must have been sleeping for hours. Pulling on his slippers, he crept silently down the stairs and slid into the kitchen.

Jimmy hid under the breakfast bar and listened in.

"Marge, we can't keep it a secret much longer," he heard his father say. "They said things would start to happen near his eleventh birthday."

"No! He will never know. He will remain here with us locked in that room if necessary," his mother argued.

Edging closer to get into a better position, Jimmy caught his arm on the radiator. He let out a small gasp.

"What was that?" his mother whispered.

Swiftly, Jimmy darted out of the space and rushed upstairs to his room, diving under the covers, pretending to be asleep.

He closed his eyes tightly as he heard the squeaking of the fifth, tenth and top steps as someone climbed the stairs. The bedroom door slowly creaked open, just enough, he imagined, to allow a beam of the landing light to illuminate his bed.

He knew it was his father who poked his head around the door; he could picture him catching his glasses on the doorframe as he did.

Jimmy could sense panic in his father as he peered in on him, as though he was worried he may have overheard something.

The door closed gently and soft slippers patted down the stairs, into the kitchen. Jimmy's mind was spinning. *What were his parents talking about? What would happen?* He thought about it a little longer before finally drifting back off to sleep.

Chapter 2

Weeks passed and Jimmy had completely forgotten about the dream and what his parents had been talking about. That was all about to change.

One day, as he was walking the usual two-mile trek to school, he saw a peculiar black crow standing in his path, almost as if it were waiting for him. This was clearly unusual, even to Jimmy's ten-year-old brain, and he side-stepped to try and avoid the confident bird. To Jimmy's surprise the crow mirrored his actions and simply hopped in front of him again. Once more Jimmy tried to walk around the crow but again it jumped in his path, giving a challenging squawk.

Feeling a little brave and pressed for time, Jimmy bent down and tried to gently nudge the bird aside with the palm of his hand. This was the wrong move. The inquisitive crow instantly became animated, squawking aggressively. The bird leapt forward, nipping Jimmy's hand. As Jimmy instinctively pulled away, the bird flew onto Jimmy's head and pecked him twice with its sharp beak. Jimmy was flailing his arms around desperately, trying to escape this unprovoked attack, until eventually the crow calmed down, jumped off of Jimmy and landed elegantly on a wooden fence. Seizing his chance, Jimmy started to run towards the school but was amazed when he saw, out of the corner of his eye, that the mysterious black crow was keeping up with him, gliding along the fence.

Slowing down to a brisk walk he glanced over his shoulder to see the crow's location. As he dreaded, it was staring at him through yellow beady eyes and was squawking in victory. Jimmy was sure the bird was laughing at him.

Jimmy's attention was drawn for only a few moments; then another squawk came from a tree to his right, then another to his left, then another, and another. Entranced by the high-pitched noise, he looked up into the trees and found a hundred more black crows almost chanting for the original, slightly fatter bird to attack again.

Confused by the surreal situation, Jimmy took a firm grip of his school bag and ran as fast as he could through the valley of chanting birds. Reaching the entrance to the school, Jimmy grabbed the giant steel gate and slammed it behind him. Looking back through the bars of the school gate he could see the determined fat little crow positioned on the path. Jimmy felt a chill of worry rush through his body, thinking whether this nemesis was going to wait for him all day. Just then the school bell reverberated and he ran through the main doors.

School was the same as any other day, with Jimmy having Art and Maths first thing.

Periodically during the lessons, Jimmy would look out of the window, firstly checking for the crow but also with the now familiar desperate feeling that there must be more to this world. Daydreaming, he hadn't noticed that he was looking towards his house. He snapped out of his trance when he saw the angry looking black cloud was hovering overhead again. Bending his neck to look at the sky above the school, he was surprised to see it was a perfect day.

"Potts, Potts, look at that dark cloud over there. That's odd, isn't it?" he frowned, shoving his elbow into the boy next to him.

Will Potts, a tall lad with brown hair parted to the side and a large protruding nose, looked from Jimmy to the area in question, and then back to Jimmy again.

"Jimmy, are you mad? I don't see a cloud in the sky! Shhh, you'll get me into trouble."

Puzzled Jimmy turned back to the area and to his surprise Potts was right; there was no cloud. It was a beautiful summer's day. *What was going on?* He thought. Then Jimmy saw it; he caught a glimpse of that crow again. The maniacal crow sitting on a tree with five others gazing directly at him, again giving him the feeling it was laughing and mocking him. Turning his head Jimmy looked away. Although he tried to ignore it, he was scared.

As the end-of-lesson bell rang, lunchtime was the next concern, not only for Jimmy but for the rest of the school children. Lunchtime was the one hour every day where Spike Williams would be unsupervised with the other children.

Spike was a full year older than Jimmy but had been kept back a year owing to his behaviour. He was a good three inches taller than Jimmy and a great deal stronger. Spike took great pleasure in pushing the younger kids about, throwing them down the small bank into the mud and taking their dinner money as a protection racket. Let's just say Spike was a mean and horrible little boy. Luckily, during this one lunchtime, Spike left Jimmy and his pal Will Potts alone and found another victim.

After lunch Jimmy followed Will and his fellow classmates into their chemistry lesson. This class always entertained Jimmy as he thought the teacher was quite mad.

The teacher, Freddy Tuft, was a small man with a slight hunch. He was very excitable and often paced up and down the classroom mumbling to himself; the other unusual thing was that he would often talk to students but remain completely focused on the ceiling. Mr. Tuft's choice of clothing also amused the students; even on the hottest of summer days he would wear a knee length brown raincoat, rich brown shoes, and carry a leather brief case, which was empty apart from his sandwiches.

As the lesson progressed Mr. Tuft started to discuss the periodic table and was going to demonstrate to the class how to make various liquids '*pop*' from inside a test tube. Mr. Tuft showed the class how it was done and then asked all the students to carefully turn on their Bunsen burners. Jimmy was very careful as he turned on the gas and ignited the bright yellow flame.

Jimmy was ready to start when he caught a glimpse out of the corner of his eye and saw twenty crows sitting in the tree directly outside the second floor classroom window. As Jimmy continued to stare at the birds he stretched his arm out in front of him to grab his science book, when a small fat wasp flew straight past his face. Instinctively, Jimmy swung out with his left arm, missed the wasp and hit the Bunsen burner onto the table. Instantly his school jumper set alight and the flame burnt straight into his left wrist.

"Sir, sir, quick Jimmy's on fire!" Will hollered frantically as the thirty students snapped their heads back to see what was going on.

In a flash Mr. Tuft grabbed a towel and threw it on Jimmy's sleeve to dampen the fire, whilst at the same time turning off the Bunsen burner. A raw sensation of fire throbbed on Jimmy's skin and the soreness was starting to burn. Mr. Tuft immediately took Jimmy to the sink and ran cold water on his wrist for five minutes before wrapping it in a clean bandage. Jimmy was told to report to the nurse for a check-up.

As Jimmy sat waiting for the nurse he still had the raw sensation of burning under the bandage. The nurse saw him quickly and she was already pulling and tugging at Mr. Tuft's bandage. Having never been to the nurse before he noticed that she was extremely tall, taller than any of the other teachers in the school and she kept grunting and sniffing. This was very odd but Jimmy thought it would be impolite to say anything. Peeling back the bandage from the skin the nurse was first to comment and noticed that the fire had left a deep mark on his forearm.

"Huumm it looks like a *9*?" the nurse mused.

Which it did, but of course from Jimmy's angle it looked more like a *6*. The nurse applied a foul smelling greasy ointment, told Jimmy to keep changing the bandages, and sent him home with a letter for his family.

Jimmy ran home and quickly told his mother the story. She was still sat in the same position as the day before, with the same stain ridden vest and piece of fried chicken resting on her stomach.

"That's interesting boy …" she said, not once moving her eyes from the daily dose of chat shows and antique programmes.

"Go and see what your father thinks, go on, scoot."

Walking into the kitchen, his wrist started to throb and after the day he'd just had he decided to go straight to bed. After a few hours of the intense soreness throughout his arm, Jimmy decided to look out of the window to see if the menacing crows were still sitting outside. To his pleasant surprise, they weren't.

Looking around the estate Jimmy saw Derek from three doors up sweeping his path with a long wooden brush. Whilst he was looking towards the council estate, there was a bump on the window that startled Jimmy.

When he looked closely at the windowsill he saw there was a small fat wasp. *Could it be the same one from earlier?* thought Jimmy. *Nah* Then … *Bump, bump, bump, bump, bump.* Five more wasps hit the window, landed on the windowsill, and sat focused on Jimmy's every movement. They sat there for a few minutes before just flying away. *That can't be normal. What a strange day.*

Later that night Jimmy explained what had happened in school to his father whilst he changed the dressing on his wrist. The family ate their tea as normal before Jimmy went back to bed.

The following morning Jimmy sluggishly rose from bed at seven a.m. and looked at the grey calendar on the wall. September 12th; three more days until his birthday, he mused. An air of excitement passed through Jimmy as he began hoping he would finally get a good present, such as a game console or a laptop. Remembering he had never received a present during the last ten years, he wondered why his parents would care now. Letting out a deep sigh he got ready for school.

Walking to school by himself once again, Jimmy anticipated seeing the black crow, but there was nothing. He breathed a sigh of relief and continued on.

Approaching the school Jimmy suddenly heard a buzzing and vibrating sound on the gentle morning breeze. He cast a sharp glance over his shoulder, but there was nothing. Shaking his head and shrugging his shoulders he carried on. Jimmy was mulling over the strange events of yesterday when from nowhere a swarm of angry wasps flew straight at him. The haze of wasps dived around his head making an aggressive '*buzzing*' noise.

"Oww! Arrgh!"

One of the raging insects had stung Jimmy on the right side of his neck.

Arrgh! What is going on? he thought.

Grabbing his neck whilst keeping his head low and trying to swat the swarm with his school bag he ran straight in to the school. As he ended the day yesterday at the nurse's office, he began today in the same fashion. Reaching the nurse's office, Jimmy nearly skidded into the surgery. Rubbing his hand against his neck, Jimmy sat on a chair. *What is going on this week?!* he thought.

After his first two lessons had finished, Jimmy started to realise it was lunchtime and time to once again avoid Spike. Little did Jimmy know that his week was going to go from bad to worse … and then to strange.

Chapter 3

Lunchtime started well enough; he had used his lunch money and picked up the last ham salad packed lunch that contained a Golden Crunch biscuit, Jimmy's favourite.

Once he and Will had eaten their food they decided to see if they could join a football match with their school friends. The only game currently being played had already started. Excited, they both joined the game and were playing for about ten minutes when for no apparent reason all the players just stopped and stood still. There was silence on the pitch and even the dropping of a pin could have been heard. What no one had noticed was that Spike had walked onto the pitch, and was threatening Steve Parkes, the owner of the football. Spike was shouting that if he could not join the game Steve would be visiting the nurse very quickly. The whole school feared Spike and moments later he was playing.

Great, no one tackles him; he won't pass, wonderful, this game is ruined! thought Jimmy. The other players also thought this but no one dared say it to him or leave the game.

Then it happened, the moment that changed Jimmy and Spike's lives forever.

Steve Parkes won the ball back with a great tackle in midfield. He beat one player, then another, and he was clear. He had Jimmy wide open on the right and Spike stood in the middle marked by two players. Naturally, through fear of repercussions, Steve took the harder option and passed to Spike. The two defenders parted like the red sea to allow Spike a clear shot at the goal. A rush of madness overcame skinny, meek Will Potts. From out of nowhere he ran at full speed and slid straight in front of Spike, cleanly taking the ball. Time stood still as the whole school stopped and gasped.

In slow motion, with the rage and power of an angry lion, Spike grabbed Will by the scruff of his neck and punched him once in the face. Falling to the ground, Will grabbed his nose to stop the blood spurting out. Spike leapt on top of Will, ready for the next assault. At that exact moment in time, seeing his friend being attacked, something happened to Jimmy; something snapped inside him. Instinctively, with anger and protective instincts pulsating through him, Jimmy rushed over, grabbed Spike by the back of his jumper and with the strength of ten bears, dragged him off of his injured friend, giving him the opportunity to jump on top of him. Spike had never been challenged in his life; he looked up in pure amazement, especially at the strength that was pinning him to the ground.

Then, as foretold, it started ...

Jimmy's eyes were pulsing bright red with the eternal fire in the pupils themselves. Slowly Spike became transfixed with the eyes and looked straight into the heart of Jimmy Threepwood's very soul. He saw a glimpse of the future; a world of destruction, free flowing fire, a cascade of ash raining down and the end of the world as we know it. This was a future too rich for a boy of twelve to handle. To Spike, it felt like an eternity gazing helplessly into those blood red fiery eyes, whilst to everyone else standing on the playground, it was seconds. Moments later Spike passed out due to the sheer magnetism of what he had seen. Seeing the huddle, Mr. Thompson ran to see what was going on.

Pushing through the crowd Mr. Thompson pointed a long, shaking finger at Jimmy. "You, boy!" he shouted, "get to the headmaster's office ... now!"

Mr. Thompson picked up Spike, who was still trembling and mumbling to himself, and rushed him to the nurse's office.

As Jimmy strolled along the corridors he couldn't understand what had happened. *Where did that strength come from?* Mostly he couldn't get the horrified look on Spike's face out of his head.

The headmaster's office was situated directly above the nurse's office and he saw Spike being carried into the surgery room. The door was open and Jimmy moved around and crouched on the stairs to look through the white railings; Spike was sitting on the edge of the bed, looking straight at the outside wall. He was as white as a ghost. Rocking back and forth, Spike kept repeating, "I've seen it, the end! Flying black horses with the wings of a bat being ridden by a horned warrior throwing lightning ... I've seen it, the ..." With that the door was slammed shut.

Moments later the headmaster's assistant summoned Jimmy to explain what had occurred moments before. Jimmy wasn't in the office long before he was sent home with the headmaster telling him he would be ringing ahead to speak with his parents.

When Jimmy walked into his house he was surprised to find his mother had moved from the chair and was standing in the kitchen.

In her normal gritty voice, caused through years of smoking, she said to him, "Your father is painting the spare bedroom, keep out of our way, he will cook dinner later."

With that, Marge waddled back to the living room and Jimmy walked upstairs to receive his punishment from his father. Jimmy kept his head down as he entered the room to speak with his father–but nothing. Jimmy's father simply greeted him and questioned him about what he wanted for tea. Nothing about the incident in school at all. *How strange. That was odd? Better not mention it ... Best to keep quiet.*

The following day at school Jimmy sat with his school year in the grand hall at 8:15 a.m. for the weekly assembly. This was near the headmaster's office and had a cold wooden floor, which each student was expected to sit on with their legs crossed and mouths closed.

The headmaster himself, Mr. Riding, a tall balding man with brown streaks of hair and square glasses, conducted the assembly.

"Students, I have some unfortunate news for you all. One of your classmates Spike Williams had some form of breakdown yesterday and has sadly been taken out of school until further notice. Please give any get well cards or messages to the school secretary who will pass them on to Spike."

From that moment on it seemed a weight had lifted from each of the students and a smile started to slowly form on all of their faces. No longer would the students be bullied and terrified during lunch times. No longer would their games be ruined; Jimmy Threepwood would be a hero to all.

For the rest of the day he was treated as one. He was congratulated, received handshakes and even got a kiss from one of the girls. The most thankful, though, was his best friend Will Potts.

"I owe you one for yesterday Jimmy. I thought that was the end of me!"

"Why did you do it, Will?" replied Jimmy.

"I don't know, it was sort of a rush of blood, but I'm glad I did and the bloody nose was worth it. We are free at last! Jimmy the hero!"

To Jimmy's surprise even some of the teachers gave him a congratulating wink and a pat on the back. He really had done a good deed ... if only they knew what was to follow.

Chapter 4

Jimmy was awoken early the following morning by an ear piercing, heartrending shrill, as though a thousand screaming souls were giving their last breath in the mortal world. The deathly noise stirred Jimmy's stomach as he pulled across his bed covers, knelt on his bed, and tore back the curtains to see what was happening. Jimmy was certain the noise had echoed from the council estate, but all he could see was an illuminating purple light flashing from the brick wall.

Calming down, Jimmy regained his composure and suddenly realised today was his eleventh birthday. He smiled to himself and was just in the motion of jumping from his bed when out of the corner of his eye he saw a slight flicker of movement inside the purple light. Pressing his face firmly on the window to get a greater view, he was sure he could make out a black shadow moving from within the darkness and slowly, eerily, it seemed to glide towards his house.

With his face squashed tightly against the window, each breath fogged the glass and every time he used his sleeve and rapidly wiped the window the shadow moved slightly closer to his house.

As the darkness drew closer Jimmy suddenly had a clear view and it was obvious that this was no shadow. This was some form of hollow skeletal figure inside a lengthy black, dishevelled, shredded cloak with a black hood casting a shadow over the face. Jimmy was transfixed and frantically moved around his bed to get a better angle or find a position where he might be able to see through one of the tears in the figure's cloak; but there wasn't one.

A metal scythe gleamed in the morning sunlight and as Jimmy looked at the hand he saw there was no flesh; just sharp yellow, bony talons firmly gripping the full length wooden handle of an immensely sharp weapon. Silently, deadly, the figure glided over the path, coming closer and closer to Jimmy's house.

Jimmy continued to stare, mesmerised by the creature as it approached his front gate. As the figure slowly turned, a second, much smaller creature came into view. The second creature was standing directly behind the first, carrying its cloak, almost as though it were trying to stop it getting dirty from the floor. The hideous knee-high, green goblin took one hand away from the cloak and stroked its shoulder length slimy black hair out of its eyes. Jimmy's gaze was averted from the sinister looking goblin by movement under the cloak of the hellish figure. Scrunching his eyes, Jimmy could see hundreds and hundreds of cockroach type creatures frantically scuttling around where his feet should have been. Somehow the air also looked different. Behind the ghastly figure was some kind of yellow odour or gas lingering in the air. For the first time Jimmy noticed that all of the flowers the figure had glided over were slowly withering, drying up, and dying. As he looked further away in the direction the creature had come from the flowers were starting to rejuvenate themselves.

The creature raised his left decaying hand and with a snap of the wrist, the gate flung open. Jimmy continued to watch in pure amazement, but then ducked quickly when the goblin looked upward in his direction and gave a sly grin; revealing its sharp, yet pointy, yellow teeth.

Breathing deeply Jimmy launched himself off of the bed and as quietly as he could ran down the stairs into the kitchen, sliding under the breakfast bar. This was instantly followed by a heavy '*RASP*' on the wooden door. Looking up, Jimmy could see that in the area where the thump had come from a dark round wet patch started forming on the door. The patch became wetter and wetter until the wood blistered and withered before his eyes. '*RASP!*' This time the patch began to creak and little brown maggots pushed through the wood, beginning to crawl though the wasting damaged panels and dropping one by one to the floor. Jimmy's father appeared in the kitchen in a fluster, trembling all over. He rushed to the door. His hand was violently shaking by the time he pulled down the handle.

The creature pushed past Jimmy's father and glided confidently and silently through the kitchen. The creature hovered by Jimmy, who was still hiding under the breakfast bar. Jimmy tried to move further back, almost burrowing into the wall, when he came face to face with the short female goblin. The goblin glanced at Jimmy, snarled, biting its teeth together before turning its nose up and continuing on into the living room.

A deep, deathly, commanding voice thundered, "You were told to make sure he was ready!"

"M-M-M-Master, I was just about to … to do it!" said Marge in a quivering voice.

Jimmy had never heard her like this.

"I, I, I … d-d-did as you said; he has no real friends or pets and spends most of his time alone!"

"Good, you have fulfilled our deal. You will not be taken as foretold, but granted an extra ten years here to waste and create misery. Make sure the boy is ready for six p.m."

Confidently turning, the creature flung its cape behind him, nearly knocking over the goblin in the process, and glided out of the house without saying another word.

Jimmy had no idea what was going on and ran upstairs when the coast was clear. He could hear his mother and father whispering, and shortly afterwards, heard his father creeping up the stairs.

"Dad, what was that?" Jimmy asked fearfully.

With a faint smile and a look of sheer disheartenment, his father sat beside him on the bed.

"Jimmy, I'm so sorry, your mother made a deal with that man, um, thing when you were born. It appeared in the hospital when I was asleep and showed your mother the future. It said she would die this year today unless she made a deal. The deal was to keep you unhappy, separated from friends with no attachments and on this day, your eleventh birthday, he would take you away to fulfil your purpose."

"What purpose?" snapped Jimmy; tears pooled in his eyes as he thought about what his father had told him. How could his mother have made a deal like that?

"I don't know, your mother would never tell me," said Jimmy's father, a tear slowly trickling down his cheek.

"Jimmy I-I'm sorry, we have to let you go, but he told us we can still see you …" he mumbled, wiping the tears away.

"Come on Jimmy, it's your birthday, let's go out for a little while. We have a few hours yet."

Those few hours disappeared in an instant and Jimmy was standing outside his steel front gate when he glanced down at his watch. 5:55 p.m.

"I'm so, so scared Dad, where am I going? What's going to happen to me?" he asked as his lower lip started to quiver and tears filled his vision.

"You'll be okay Jimmy; they wouldn't have done all this just to harm you." Jimmy's dad stepped in to hold his son but stopped himself. He knew the deal; he knew what would happen if Jimmy was loved.

The front gate started to vibrate and looking off to the right Jimmy could see the air distorting, as though he was staring at leaking gas. A short, sharp hiss of lightning crackled in the air, followed by a burst of purple light and smoke. From nowhere the creature and its foul companion appeared.

"Time is short, follow me, now!" roared the abomination, sending a chill down the spine of both Jimmy and Bill Threepwood.

Desperately scared and unable to control his trembling body Jimmy followed. Walking alongside the dirty brown-cloaked goblin, Jimmy constantly looked back over his shoulder at his father who was just frozen on the spot staring at his son walking off.

"That is my servant Xanadu; she is my assistant in all matters. Now quickly, we have others to collect!"

Jimmy glanced at Xanadu, but was more interested in looking at the creature and the multitude of bugs and insects slithering under his cloak. He also noticed that ordinary people in their path couldn't see them, but suddenly gained the overwhelming urge to cross the road away from them. Those who didn't cross the road were suddenly overcome by a wave of illness; one of them nearly collapsed and had to hold a fence for support. Like the flowers, once the creature was a short distance away, they became well again.

Moments passed and the group was now approaching the council estate hiding under the shadow of the mysterious black cloud hanging overhead. Jimmy saw the two-storey council flat with a large brick wall facing them in front of which was a small circular green. Approaching the centre of the wall, the creature raised its scythe and thumped the wall three times. Instantly a dark purple glow of light formed in the shape of a door and the wall crumbled to dust and rubble. Grabbing Jimmy's arm with a thin, bony, skeleton hand the creature pulled him through. Jimmy's eyes were burning in the bright light but his body was freezing cold, with each breath he took forming a puff of condensation. Jimmy couldn't see anything but felt the eerie presence of evil and darkness rising within.

Chapter 5

Stepping into the dazzling purple light, Jimmy immediately felt an eerie chill submerge his body. Shaking and folding his arms to retain the last bit of heat, he breathed as his lungs felt the icy artic air circulating in his chest. Each breath felt cold and uncomfortable as white puffs of condensation floated wastefully into the air. The ground felt like solid smooth marble and in the distance Jimmy could see a light, a door maybe, but definitely a light, projecting the path forward.

After only a few moments and a brisk pace the group reached the light and again Jimmy was dragged through it. Closing his eyes and trying to hold back the fear, Jimmy stepped forward into the unknown.

Breathing deeply, his foot touched the floor but to his surprise he heard the crunch of dead, dry leaves and the snap of an old wooden branch. Opening his eyes Jimmy was standing in the middle of a forest. This was a small open section and had tall dark trees circling a bare grassy area and a yellow and orange flamed fire was roaring in the centre.

Carefully positioned around the fire were five bulky wooden tree stumps, formerly grand trees cut down to create seats. The forest air continued to send an icy chill down Jimmy's spine; he was terrified, hearing the noises of wolves howling, birds pecking, bushes rustling and insects crawling all around him. Petrified, he pulled his arms across his trembling body as his eyes darted in every direction. Stepping forward, the back of the fire came into view and there, once again, sat the fat black crow that had stalked his every move. Jimmy walked toward the crow. He was within touching distance and glanced over his shoulder to ask the cloaked creature why it was following him when '*Puff!*' a short sharp snap was followed by a cloud of dark purple smoke. The sound startled Jimmy and sent his heart racing. As the smoke receded Jimmy slowly made out the figure of a man.

"Finally we meet in person, Jimmy Threepwood. I have been watching you for a great many years; you have been a great enigma to me. You don't act like the others," mused the tall, black haired, grey bearded man dressed in an elegant blood red robe. His voice was deep and grisly, almost cutting.

Jimmy's eyes were diverted from his wrinkled, dry face to an entrancing fist sized red crystal hanging from his neck. As Jimmy stared into the stone he was startled as a face appeared, screaming back at him.

Snapping out of his trance Jimmy immediately and sharply turned his nose and screwed up his face. *Wow, he smells of rotting flesh and his face, it looks like it's slowly decaying*, he thought.

"My name is Lyreco, and this is the Elksidian Forest."

There was a rustle of leaves near where Jimmy had appeared and in a gut wrenching eerie voice, the hooded creature lurking in the darkness spoke.

"My time here is done. The others have also been collected and will arrive shortly," it said coldly.

With a sharp turn, the cloaked creature raised his scythe. Jimmy glared at Xanadu, who simply returned a foul look and a grimace. In an instant they were gone. The egress was more spectacular than Lyreco's entrance;

with the creature almost sucked through a tiny hole in the air into what Jimmy could only assume was a different dimension.

The instant the tiny vortex disappeared the whole forest seemed to rumble. Simultaneously three dark purple doors opened in thin air and three children stepped into the forest with the light fading behind them. There were two boys and one girl that Jimmy couldn't take his eyes off. Her piercing green eyes glowed in the light of the flame.

"Good, you have all arrived safety, my name is Lyreco and I am a Dark Reaver, please take a seat," said the cloaked creature, gesturing to each of the thick wooden trunks around the fire; one by one the children sat themselves down.

"The creatures whom you all just met were the Gatekeeper, and his minion Xanadu. The Gatekeeper controls the walkways between life and death. The Gatekeeper knows when the mortals will die and he is ready to greet their souls. The Gatekeeper either sends them upwards to the eternal paradise, or ... well, enough of that; I bet you are wondering what is going on here."

Jimmy looked at the other three children and he noticed that they all had something in common; they all had some sort of edge, some sort of dark spirit or aura shrouding them. It was enough for Jimmy to feel uneasy about the situation, and although he would never admit it, he was scared.

Lyreco started.

"My young apprentices, it is written that the world will continue to evolve over time and mankind evolves with the increase in technology, and demands on the planet drain the resources. Each passing decade the planet dies a little more, until one day it will be gone. It is foretold by the Elders that every two millennia our Dark Lord and Master Tyranacus will rise from the ashes and destroy all life on the planet.

"But, only four powerful beings that own the mark of Tyranacus have the combined power to bring him to his destiny. Two millennia ago four such youths who possessed the mark were brought to this very Forest and trained in all manner of powers, magic and weapons until they eventually gained the power to open the gates. The four warriors and our lord master purged this planet and reduced it to fire and rubble.

"There were of course, as there always is, a meddlesome bunch that tried to stop it, but they were no match. Once the destruction was complete the four warriors took their place as rulers of the planet and formed the re-birth in their own form. That of course was a long time ago and now that time has come again.

"You were all born consecutively on the 12th, 13th, 14th, and 15th of September and all wear the mark of Tyranacus, is that correct?"

Glancing around the group, scared of what might happen, Jimmy nodded.

"Ya ... Ya ... Yes, sir."

This was immediately followed by two further nods. But from the last youth, nothing, just silence. Rising from the stump a youth with spiky dyed brown hair shouted, "Are you real? What is this rubbish? Rising dark lords, powers, destruction, it's all rubbish, I'm going."

With trepidation Jimmy looked at the youth then snapped back to Lyreco and he could see the blood draining from his already cold decaying face. Lyreco rose, pulled aside his cloak, and pointed his long, stick thin finger at the spiky haired boy, quivering in anger. Immediately the boy reacted, thrusting his hands over his mouth and dropping to his knees, with tears streaming from his eyes. The youth slowly turned to the rest of the group and they gasped. The youth moved his hands from his mouth and they could see it had been covered over with a rubbery flesh which stretched as he tried to scream.

"YOU WILL DO AS YOU ARE TOLD, BOY!" demanded Lyreco.

With a further wave of his hand the boy was levitated from the floor and dropped back onto the wooden stump. With a wheeze, Lyreco lowered his finger and his mouth returned to normal.

"Let that be the first lesson to you all. I will teach you the powers you need and you will far eclipse me, but for now YOU WILL DO AS YOU ARE TOLD!"

The brown haired male looked sheepishly at the other children, and then looked at the floor.

"Now you know I demand respect, show me your marks."

Without complaint and with haste all four youths rolled up their sleeves and revealed the number 9 to Lyreco and a 6 to each other as they looked across the line.

"Good, now the training can begin," said Lyreco. "Your training has many areas and one day you will have the power of the gods, but first we must see what your inner power tells us. You, Threepwood, stand and walk to the fire."

Reluctantly Jimmy rose and sauntered to the crackling yellow flame. The radiating heat could be felt pulsing from the source. Lyreco started chanting some unusual words and in a flash the flame illuminated and roared bright green.

"Place your hand in the flame."

Scared stiff and in fear of what would happen if he didn't, Jimmy raised his right arm, looked at Lyreco, looked at the three youths, and then plunged his arm straight into the centre. To his amazement there was no pain, just a warm sensation of floating and intense burning.

Opening his eyes he was startled to find he was floating high in the air above the fire. He saw his body had become alight with intense surging flames. He flapped both hands and he started rise up and up until he found himself level with the shortest tree. The jaws of the other kids had dropped to the floor. In front of their very eyes the boy known as Threepwood had turned into a bird drenched in fire and was drifting off into the sky.

With one swift movement of Lyreco's hand Threepwood's flames perished and gravity dragged him crashing down to the ground with a thud. Picking himself up and dusting off the dirt he saw the rest of the group were staring intently.

Unusual, I have never heard of a student having the inner power of a Phoenix, how strange, thought Lyreco, rubbing his beard.

"You, Harry Hopkins, you're next," speaking to the formerly overconfident spiky-haired male.

Without saying a word and showing no fear, Harry plunged his right arm into the green fire and with a bright flash of brilliant light he was gone. There in his place was a venomous black viper, slithering and rustling on the forest floor. The smooth skinned serpent glared at Jimmy, slowly opened his mouth to reveal two pointed razor sharp fangs, and gave a sinister hiss. Again, Lyreco raised his hand and once the haze of smoke levelled, Harry reappeared, shaking off the curious feeling.

Next to put their hand in the fire was the third male. He was taller than Jimmy with shaved blond hair and a large distinguished nose, and Jimmy thought he had a menacing look about him. In front of Jimmy's eyes this male, Percy Timmins re-appeared as a gigantic blue and yellow dragon. Timmins swung his scaled neck toward Lyreco, looked him up and down, before firing a rage of yellow fire at him from his extensive jaw. Lyreco simply held up his arm in a blocking motion and the fire parted in mid-air. Once he'd had enough, Lyreco clenched his fist, drawing the magic out of Timmins as he morphed back into human form and fell straight to the floor. Timmins kept his head down as if expecting his punishment, but it never came. Lyreco gave an evil smile and requested Timmins sit back down.

Finally, Talula Airheart stood up to the fire and morphed into a black bat with glowing red eyes and a ferocious snap. The creature gave a mighty cry, before changing quietly back to the human form.

"Good, now we have seen your inner power I suggest your first lesson will be to practise them. You can change to these forms at any time, but as you can see by the way you are feeling now, they will take a lot of your energy and may leave you defenceless. Once you master the power no one will be able to stop you, not even me.

"Practise your powers and I shall return."

PUFF!

A purple cloud of smoke filled the forest air, releasing a pungent smell of burnt sulphur. From within the cloud came an almighty squawk and out soared the familiar fat black crow into the night sky.

Chapter 6

Once alone, the group stared at each other in sheer disbelief. Returning to a natural flickering yellow flame, the fire produced enough light to keep the night creatures at bay.

Harry Hopkins was the first to move. He crunched over the dry leaves and dead twigs, approaching Jimmy, and aggressively shoved him on the right shoulder.

"What's your story? I think you're in the wrong place, out of my way. I'm gonna learn how to turn into that snake again and see what happens if I bite you." His tone was arrogant and selfish.

Harry Hopkins shoved past Jimmy and stood behind the stump, and closing his eyes, he tried to summon the creature. Jimmy started to feel disheartened until a gentle sweet smelling fragrance meandered past his nose and a gentle hand squeezed his shoulder.

A soft voice spoke.

"Don't worry about him, he's an idiot. I loved that fire bird, how did you do that? By the way, I'm Talula."

Jimmy turned and smiled at the girl with shoulder length brown hair and bright green eyes. Talula smiled back, but something wasn't quite right. Jimmy immediately noticed there was no warmth within her face or eyes. She was ice cold.

"Hello, I'm Jimmy; I-I-I don't know how I did that with the bird? It just happened?"

Smiling again, Talula said, "I'm glad to be here, anything to get away from my father. He used to lock my bedroom door and leave me there for days. It was some agreement with that ma ... creature who brought us here."

Jimmy could see the sadness and hatred in Talula's eyes, but he knew instantly he was different. He didn't resent his mother for her behaviour and he loved his father; but clearly for Talula it had been much worse.

"I'm going to try and turn into that bat again; it was fun!" With that Talula walked off with Jimmy's eyes still following her.

The third boy was already standing alone, facing away from the group and looking into the darkness of the forest. Jimmy considered talking to him, but thought better of it.

Jimmy and the rest of the group spent the next few hours trying as hard as they could to morph into their mythical creatures, but it just didn't seem to work. Had there been any passers-by they would surely have commented on how odd the four children looked, standing in the middle of a forest at night, mumbling to themselves.

Jimmy started thinking about his childhood and his own life, in the hope that he might overcome the boredom and his dwelling on what Talula had said. As far back as he could remember his mother had been horrible to him. She had ignored him and regularly sent him to his room. She had difficulty in moving due to her excessive weight and rarely left the house. When they did go out for a family meal she would often just sit there and order everything off the menu and rarely talk to Jimmy. Then there was his dad; he was a kind man, but very weak. His wife bullied him and it was only when he was alone with Jimmy that he showed his caring, compassionate side. As Jimmy thought about his father and some of the fun they had had, a feeling of warmth ignited in his stomach. The burning sensation reappeared and as he focused on his surroundings he found he was floating high above Elksidian Forest, illuminating the night sky.

Effortlessly he flew, circling higher, then lower, leaving a trail of bright flames in his wake which gently fizzled out in the night air.

He dived, plummeting like a meteor towards the fire pulling up at the last minute as he burst through the top of the roaring flames, sending a plume of smoke into the air. In all his euphoria he had completely forgotten about his companions and, looking down, he saw the others glaring in envy with anger strewn across their faces that he was the first to realise his power.

As the anger mounted in front of his eyes they also transformed into their respective creatures. *That's odd*, thought Jimmy, *they struggled for hours, but that look of pure rage and envy and they have all suddenly changed. It can't be …*

A flurry of chilled air thrust past his face. The large blue and yellow dragon appeared, ferociously flapping his clawed wings, flying dangerously close to him. The wind from its humongous wingspan was forcing the smaller phoenix backward even with Jimmy flapping frantically.

The dragon stopped and hovered effortlessly before Jimmy and growled, "I am the strongest of you all, feel my POWER!"

The forceful dragon wrenched its immense jaws open and a spittle of fire started formulating at the back of its throat. In anticipation Jimmy closed his eyes and waited for the impact. Suddenly, the air was filled by an ear-piercing shriek. Jimmy opened his eyes and saw that

Talula, in the form of a bat, had flown at Percy's eye and they were now both intertwined with fire spurting upward into the air. A rush of blood flooded over Jimmy. He lowered his head and charged with all his might at the oversized dragon. With an almighty collision the three were sent into an uncontrollable tailspin and nosedived towards the forest floor. As Jimmy was spinning at an incredible speed he thought he noticed the dark outline of a deathly black castle in the near distance being rained on by streams of intense purple lightning. The next thing he remembered was seeing the ground coming closer and closer ... and then there was impact. All three hit the floor in a heap and morphed back to their normal forms.

Eventually, Jimmy awoke to find the others perched on their respective trunks.

"Ah, the last to rise. You all had quite the fall! You cannot be hurt here. This is an enchanted wood, made specifically for training. Percy's fire will not hurt you. Nor will the venomous bite of Harry's fangs; you are safe to practise as you will!" said Lyreco, almost as if he were enjoying the fighting and suffering.

Rubbing his neck and stiff shoulder, Jimmy bowed his head and slowly walked to his seat. As he sat down he looked at Lyreco.

"Master, what is the castle in the distance?"

Lyreco smiled.

"Well spotted, Jimmy," he commented, looking disappointedly at the others. "That is Sepura Castle, and one day it will be your home. However, the doors have been sealed for over a millennium. Once your powers increase and you possess the Amulet of Trident, entry will be granted to the mysteries of the old and the scrolls of the previous four who also bore the mark of Tyranacus."

In excitement, Percy shouted, "What is the Amulet of Trident, Master?"

"All in good time, my students, all in good time," replied Lyreco.

"I believe you have now all learnt the secret of how to morph into your inner creatures. The secret to the power is rage, anger, fury, jealousy," said the teacher, becoming more and more excited with each word. "The more anger that channels through your body, the greater the power at your disposal ..."

But that's not what happened to me, thought Jimmy. *I was thinking about my father, some of the good times we have had. I wasn't angry at all. Is there something wrong with me? Perhaps Harry was right, maybe I shouldn't be here.*

Lyreco continued, "... You are ready for the next lesson, but for now you will need to sleep."

Percy Timmins was sitting on the edge of his seat, looking like he would burst when he shouted in excitement, "I don't want to sleep! I'm ready for more!"

Jimmy turned to Percy. *He seemed so quiet earlier, but he is just power mad and greedy, I don't want to get in his way.* Lyreco grimaced at the group.

"No more! You will sleep and be ready for tomorrow." Lyreco waved his hand at the fire, instantly extinguishing it as a sheet of darkness covered the forest.

Chapter 7

Jimmy awoke to find the others staring down at him. Whilst regaining focus he looked back at them and could almost feel their thoughts; *you're worthless, what a waste of time*. These, of course, weren't their actual thoughts, these were the thoughts his mother had implanted since birth. However, Jimmy knew they were thinking something similar about him.

Standing up, he stretched his arms and found that his back was hurting from sleeping on the cold, damp hard ground all night. As he finished his stretches, out of thin air Lyreco appeared holding packages in crinkly brown paper, bound with string.

"My students, I have a gift for you all!"

Lyreco gently tossed the four packages into the air and levitated them with little effort displayed. With a pushing motion the packages floated to each of the students, who were waiting eagerly.

The students tore open the packages, revealing a black, hooded robe with a soft purple velvet lining. The robe was made of material that none of the students had ever felt or seen and was completely weightless. On the right breast of each cloak was a hand-embroidered symbol. Percy looked down and his was a powerful blue and yellow dragon, Harry's a predatory black viper. Looking at his, Jimmy noticed for the first time that his inner power seemed to be different to the others. His was a beautiful golden yellow phoenix, a peaceful bird, not like the other aggressive and dark creatures, but Jimmy just shrugged it off.

Swinging the robe over his shoulders Jimmy immediately felt a surge of dark energy resonate throughout his body and electricity sparked from the end of his fingers tips. A veil of darkness flooded over Jimmy. His eyes began to pulse with a blood red intensity and, gazing around the forest, he could see hundreds of ghostly outlines kneeling before him, clawing at his legs.

Looking at the others, Jimmy saw that their eyes were also pulsing bright red, when suddenly he jolted and felt a massive build-up of energy getting stronger and stronger from within him. The power was resonating throughout his stomach, along his arms and neck until he could no longer bear it. In an involuntary thrusting motion, unable to contain the power any longer, he flung his arms forward and a tsunami of intense light surged from his arms out of his clenched fists and absorbed into a defenceless nearby tree. The power had illuminated the whole of his arms and that of his companions. Seconds later, all four children dropped to the floor in exhaustion.

Barely able to lift his head Jimmy saw four thin, lifeless black ash silhouettes in the shape of a tree. Seconds later all four trees just crumbled with the weight of the gentle breeze. *Wow, what was that?* he thought.

Smiling, Lyreco looked at his students, having had their first real exposure to the raw power. "These are the first of many items you will need to become all-powerful; the rest will come in time through challenges and quests. But for now I have a surprise for you all, I have some people I want you to meet; some of you have already had the pleasure of meeting them."

Lyreco turned his cloak with an introductory gesture and out of the distant dark woods staggered two figures that Jimmy knew very well.

First out of the wooded area stepped Freddy Tuft, Jimmy's science teacher whom he found so amusing in his Chemistry lessons. The teacher still had his hunch and wore that comical knee length brown coat and had his briefcase. The next figure was Jimmy's old school nurse. She was still huge and wore her nurse's uniform. Freddy Tuft stepped forward.

"Morning students, morning Jimmy, it's been a while since we have seen you."

Jimmy looked at them both in amazement. *What is going on? Am I dreaming this? Surely these two couldn't be here ... could they?*

Freddy Tuft took another step forward and a voice echoed from his stomach.

"We've been in this suit far too long!"

Freddy grabbed a piece of skin on the left hand side of his neck and literally pulled his face off to reveal a little green head with bright yellow eyes blinking and peering back. Tuft then mumbled downward, "Your turn!"

A green slimy hand punched its way out of Tuft's stomach, pushing green ooze and yellow pus into the air that released a foul smelling green gas. The hand pulled swiftly downward and then upward, which caused Tuft's body to split in half and fall off like a coat from a hanger. What remained were two slimy, slippery green toad-like creatures with yellow eyes and a horn in the centre of their heads. They were both supporting a wooden frame with one balanced on top of another.

The creature on the top jumped to the floor and landed in a heap. The second quickly discarded the frame, which had, until moments ago, supported the artificial body of Freddy Tuft, Jimmy's former Chemistry teacher. Jimmy's jaw and that of his fellow students hit the floor. On cue the giant nurse stepped forward, tugged aggressively at what seemed to be a rubber coating, and completely tore off her skin to reveal an angry looking giant bald ogre with one big green eye in the middle of its head. The ogre had a hairy body, with a brown waistcoat, black trousers and knee length black boots. *That's why he kept mumbling to himself, he needed to tell the other one when to move? And that's why the nurse was such a giant ... it all makes sense!* thought Jimmy.

The ogre stood and scratched under its left arm, pulled something green out and stuck it in its mouth and started to chew. The Ogre, still chewing whatever it was, put its arm behind its back and produced a massive, clearly extensively used stone club before proceeding to smash a nearby rock to pieces.

"Ah, it feels good to stretch my muscles. I've been in that rubber suit far too long!"

The slimy green creature that had previously been Mr. Tuft's head licked his lips, revealing a lizard like bright pink tongue, and hissed

"Morning studentsssss, we will be your initial mentors for the forthcoming monthsssss. I am Iveco, I will *sssshow* you the wonders of demonic *attackssss*; this is Idlewhich, my brother," the creature pointed to its companion, "he will teach you the art of chaos, poison and using deception as a weapon, *ssss*. This is LaForte," Iveco grinned, pointing to the ogre. "He will teach you how to conjure powerful alliessss to assist you in your battlessss. A very powerful conjurer he issss."

LaForte closed his large eye and concentrated for a few seconds. A stomach curdling screech followed and out from the soil in front of the group grew a human sized toad warrior holding a square red shield, a razor sharp sword, and what appeared to be a Viking helmet. LaForte raised his monumental right finger in the direction of the group and the warrior stomped forward, swinging its blade with every step. The warrior got within a foot of the group and LaForte lowered his finger. The warrior was slowly sucked body first into the ground, disappearing before the students' very eyes. Giving a satisfied smile Iveco said,

"This training will see you well towards your next step ..."

The basic initial training began over the next few weeks with all students adapting very well. However, little was ever explained as to why they were there, why they were being trained, and for what purpose. But the students didn't dare to question the tutors through fear of repercussion. During the first few weeks the students learned the art of poison and how to create it from forest berries, foliage, and mud. The students all managed to create a reasonable brew except Talula, who seemed to have some sort of sixth sense. Talula somehow knew to add more Boyant leaf, chop the ankle nut at an angle, and add simple ground mud. This immensely increased the potency of her potions. During one case the excess fumes floated up a nearby tree. One whiff for a bird dozing on a branch and that was it; it died on the spot and plummeted to the ground. Talula had no idea how she knew to add the extra items, but she did.

Percy Timmins took to the deception and chaos lessons very well. After only a few verbal training classes the group was sent to a major well-known city centre with the task of obtaining a precious metal ring with a rare golden diamond.

The popular city centre contained well-branded local shops mixed with major chains, bakeries, cafes, and toyshops. What was also apparent was that this was a busy city, covered by CCTV and regular police patrols. The only briefing the youths had was to use their skills to get the precious item, but they were only given one chance. If they failed, they would be returned to the Forest.

Percy decided he wanted to sit back and watch the events unfold, so he found a small bush directly opposite the Diamond Buy jewellers in a low coverage spot for the CCTV.

Unsurprisingly, Harry Hopkins decided to meet the challenge head on. Deciding he had a plan, he grabbed Talula and explained what they were going to do. Harry reinforced the fact that for the plan to work it would take two people and she was helping whether she liked it or not. Percy and Jimmy waited as the plan unfolded. The plan was very simple. Talula would enter the store and speak to the lone shop worker, distracting him whilst Harry leant over the counter, picked up a ring and walked out. Moments later he would return, wait behind Talula and approach the shopkeeper informing him that he had bought the stolen ring a few moments before, it was the wrong size and that he wanted to exchange it for the golden ring. Little did Harry know that the instant he leant over the counter and slid across the rear glass panel, the alarm would be set off. Both Harry and Talula's hearts sank as they were engulfed in the loud ringing alarm. Seconds later, the alarm stopped and the shopkeeper was frozen in place.

Idelwhich's voice could be heard echoing through the air. "Very disappointing."

They were both snapped back to the forest. The shopkeeper unfroze and was none the wiser after a short-term memory erasure.

Jimmy decided enough was enough and thought about using props. He bought a briefcase and a number of magazines from a local shop. He spent a number of hours ripping up the magazines into paper currency shaped pieces. He then filled the briefcase with stacks of his fake money, placing real money only on the top to create the illusion that the case was full of real money. He entered the store, talked to the shopkeeper, and pretended to be from a considerably rich background.

He pointed to the mystical ring and showed the shopkeeper the money. The shopkeeper was duly excited about the expensive sale. Pretending that his phone was ringing, Jimmy left the store, locking the briefcase. When he returned he explained to the shopkeeper that his girlfriend, who was waiting in a nearby hairdresser, wanted to see the ring before purchase. Jimmy explained that if he were allowed to take the ring he would leave the locked briefcase full of money. Excited, the shopkeeper agreed, but as Jimmy stepped out of the shop the shopkeeper shouted after him

"Hang on a minute; I want to double check that money!"

Time instantly froze and Jimmy was cast back to the forest, branded as a failure.

Remaining in his secure spot, Percy saw the events unfold and continued to watch the shopkeeper, waiting patiently, soundlessly. Whilst watching the shopkeeper he noticed a number of bad habits. On two occasions the shopkeeper put his hand in the till and took money, placing it into his pocket. The shopkeeper would then close the shop when it was supposed to be open and walk two doors down to the local public house and spend his illegal gains in there. Whilst he was in the public house Percy slithered to the shop and found a number of interesting facts. The first was that the shop was supposed to be open all day and second, the shopkeeper didn't own the store, in fact the owner was Grantly White of Diamond Buy Holdings Limited. Percy gave an evil victorious grin. Percy grabbed a pen and a little piece of paper and wrote a small note.

Dear Mr. White,

I have been observing your shop for a number of days and notice that your shopkeeper has been removing money from your till and then closing the store to attend the local public house. He then returns to the shop intoxicated and often falls asleep.

May I suggest you check the recent till transactions and conduct an on the spot visit.

Yours sincerely,

P.T.

On top of the perfectly written letter was a further, smaller note.

This is a copy of a letter that will be sent to Mr. White and you will undoubtedly lose your job. That is unless you take the golden coloured ring from the cabinet, put it in a red box with a bow and place it in front of the bush opposite the store. How you cover your tracks for the loss of the ring is your decision.

When the shopkeeper returned and read the note his heart sank. "I can't lose this job, it's all I have," he mumbled to himself, a small bead of sweat dripping slowly down his forehead. His next thought was how he would cover the loss; a few missing hundreds were easy to hide, he supposed.

Defeated, he packaged the ring as requested and left it in the required spot, looking around to see who had caught him. As the shopkeeper walked off he once again froze in his place along with all the other consumers and with a '*puff*' Percy was back in the forest, victorious.

"Ha-ha marvellous! Now you three, this is how it's done. Not only did Percy get the item, the shopkeeper gave it to him, put a bow on it and hid the loss himself. Ha-ha! Percy never even entered the shop, PERRRRFECT ...”

Iveco approached Percy and gave him a wink. He then held the golden ring in the palm of his hands and whispered a mysterious chant. Iveco handed the ring to Percy as the prize for the victory and Percy reciprocated with a nod of appreciation. Unsuspectingly Percy placed the ring on his right index finger and immediately started reacting. His eyes and the ring glazed over pure black. Seconds later Percy snapped back to reality to see Iveco smiling.

“Percy, your prize for this success is the legendary ring of vision. Now that it is activated you are given a few seconds’ glimpse of the future. This will give you the immense power to see if your deceptions will work. Hold that ring dear to you; you will draw upon it in the very near future.” With that Iveco turned and walked off into the woods.

The training continued for a further few weeks until Iveco decided to teach the class how to use demonic attacks. All four students were taken to the far side of the forest where Iveco had prepared an ample firing range, setting up a series of human shaped targets made out of hay and corn bags at the far end. The bags took the form of creepy, soulless scarecrows standing in a line, however Iveco had enchanted them and they were trudging like zombies in the distant area. Iveco focused his eyes on one of the moving objects. Pulling both hands to his waist, a pure, flaming black fireball the size of a football began to manifest. The others looked on at him in envy as he held the immense, scalding fireball in the grasp of his claws. In a flash he unleashed it and at supersonic speed it not only hit the target, it obliterated it and the other three next to it. Iveco turned to talk to the class and the obliterated fragments slowly drifted back together on the dusty floor and reformed thanks to Iveco's enchantment.

"Class, this is the raw power within you all, but something you must focus on and progress on your own. These gifts will not be given to you."

Each student stood in front of their allocated target, focused, and tried to use their demonic attack. During the first few attempts nothing happened. On the next attempt Percy managed to create a sliver of fire, which just sizzled to the floor. Iveco walked back into view.

"This power is attuned to your inner soul. You can each do a different attack, do not focus on my power, let your mind go blank, and allow the energy to be released from within."

That extra bit of information was all Harry needed, it instantly clicked. He closed his eyes and what came out of his clenched fists amazed even Iveco. Two solid continuous beams of intense burning light discharged a magnitude of power, which had the same impact as Iveco's. Harry didn't wait for the targets to reform before he released the weapon again, intending this time for the targets to be completely obliterated. Harry had quickly mastered this aggressive act, which didn't come as great surprise to the others.

Hours passed before Talula managed to perfect the technique, which fired a single devastating green fireball from her adjoined palms. This wasn't as powerful as Harry's, but useful enough. Percy fared a little better, and attuned to his inner power, producing a continuous stream of fire from both wrists. This didn't have the intensity and range of the others, but at close quarters once again disintegrated the eerie scarecrows.

For Jimmy however, there was no such luck. Jimmy spent hours practising and receiving personal training from Iveco and the others, but there was nothing. Jimmy's lack of success in all areas started to make his companions think that he certainly wasn't cut out for his destiny. The other students started to laugh at him behind his back and make jokes about him. That was apart from Talula, who as usual just kept out of it.

After a few more days of practising, Jimmy finally had some success. He held out his arm like a javelin thrower and a small electrically charged bolt appeared in his hand. Jimmy held it until the charge was ready and threw it through the air, plunging it straight into the heart of the target. A micro second later '*zzzzzeewww*' the target evaporated into dust. *Phew, thank goodness for that*, thought Jimmy, looking at his hand; it was still crackling. After finally seeing the power of his attack the others just turned away and didn't comment again.

Chapter 8

A few more days passed and the group became stronger and even more powerful. They were now able to summon their inner creatures in an instant and had learned to sustain and control them indefinitely. Their progression amazed even Lyreco, who could no longer use his own abilities to drag them out of their mystical forms.

The group sat around the spiritual fire discussing their progress when their attention was drawn to a grinding, popping sound. Turning towards the noise, they saw a black distorted diamond vortex materialise, expanding and tearing the very fabric of the mortal realm. Xanadu stepped out. The vortex compressed and started collapsing in on itself.

At the last possible second a soulless shadow thrust his upper body out of the hole, shrieking and hollering. It slammed its claws into the soft forest mud, clambering desperately whilst being dragged back to the deathly realm. The struggle intensified until, with a hiss, the vortex snapped shut, cutting the soul in half. The perished soul screamed toward the group and then evaporated into a shadowy emptiness, drifting off into the sky.

Xanadu gave a sinister chuckle, approached Lyreco's ear and whispered, "It is time. They have matured and are ready to be collected. Looks like the children are also ready. They must go now!"

In reply, Lyreco nodded. "Yes, they are ready," he confirmed.

"Group! I have great news."

All four youths, excited, but also apprehensive looked at their master.

"My students, the time has come for your first real challenge. Over the last few weeks you have learned new skills, gained a new arsenal of weaponry and have mastered the art of gaining what you want through deception and skill. But this challenge is different. You are to travel to the village of Puzzlewood and each collect a white stallion from the stables. You will bring the stallions back here unharmed and the challenge will be complete. Do you understand?"

The students looked at each other then quickly nodded in agreement.

"You will get these stallions at all cost and you must be ready to fight and destroy anyone who stands in your way. Now go, prepare yourself and I will arrange for you to be transported."

Walking to collect some items for the journey, Jimmy thought to himself, *after all our training on how to use magic, potions, and learning how to fly using our inner creatures, we are going to collect a horse?* Harry Hopkins was having the same thoughts, only he expressed his verbally.

"What a joke, a horse, *puhh*! Who is gonna stop us? You all saw what I did to that pathetic scarecrow, haha *puh* what a waste of time. I want to learn that conjuring power."

The students didn't take too long to get prepared and once they were ready they approached Lyreco, who said;

"Work together and you will succeed, work alone and you may perish."

"Master?" asked Talula inquisitively, "Why don't we all just transform and fly to the village with one of us carrying Harry?"

"Why! You have all felt the effects, you know you cannot sustain your powers for that length of journey, and even if you did you would be completely drained and fatigued on arrival. You would be defenceless!"

Reaching into his cloak Lyreco produced a pulsating, moss covered tree branch. He extended it to Percy and as the others touched it, with a crackle they were gone, sucked into the ether of time and space.

"Master," said Xanadu, "I have concerns about Threepwood. Is he really one of the four foretold to ravage this world? He seems to have an air of goodness and feeling about him."

"Yes, I agree," snarled Lyreco. "But I can see a way to end that once and for all, he won't feel anything when I have finished with him." He smiled coldly.

The group re-emerged at the entrance to the small and forgotten Shakespearian village of Puzzlewood. A picturesque village, Puzzlewood was impeccably clean with no litter anywhere in sight, with beautiful large white houses, thatched roofs and a flock of sheep roaming freely on the cobblestones. With a cloudless, red sky the village was illuminated in all its glory. Walking through the village the group one by one pulled their cowls over their heads, trying not to draw attention to themselves.

They passed a number of villagers who seemed to just nod and carry on with their business. After going a short distance and finding no sign of the stables, they decided to ask a local for directions. They approached a few people who simply put their heads down and walked that little bit faster. Percy spotted The Monument Arms. This was an oldie-worldie-style public house with a bright red crest of a monument. The group assumed the crest was the statue at the centre of the crossroads they had just passed. Entering the public house, they were surprised when instantly the music stopped and everyone turned to glare at the intruders who had dared to enter their sanctuary.

Harry took the lead and stepped forward. "Fine village folk, we search for the local stables."

The patrons moaned between themselves for a few minutes until the publican stepped from behind the counter and hobbled over to the group. The frail old landlord, who had not a single hair on his head, began mumbling;

"Alright there me o'l butt, not sharrrr you should be in these 'ere parts, I think you should go for I cal the o'l law to throw you out!"

The group simply smiled at the man and nodded. Especially as they knew they could take the roof off the establishment with a wave of their hand, but they decided to just turn and walk away.

The group continued for a few more minutes and eventually started to leave the town. Whilst walking, in the distance they could see the outline of an old wooden shack on the horizon. As they approached they were relieved to find that this shack was actually the stable and there, grazing on a luscious green grass in the paddocks, were six pure white stallions.

Climbing the waist high wooden fence each of the group felt a gentle buzzing sensation pass over their bodies as though they had just stepped through an invisible barrier. The group also smelt something wafting through the air which they could only describe as the remnants of crispy bacon or burnt sulphur.

Percy was the first to comment on the ease of the task. Arrogantly he let his guard down and momentarily distracted his companions. Their attention was drawn for only a split second when suddenly, from somewhere, *WHACK!* Turning, Percy saw Talula soar through the air, crashing back first into a black box attached to the side of the stable.

Sparks projected from the box and Talula lay unconscious on the floor. Snapping into action, the group stepped back to back and scrutinised their surroundings. For the first time they now realised they were inside a buzzing yellow bubble, which was slowly dematerialising all around them. In awe Jimmy stared around the sphere; *a perception filter. They really exist, wow.*

"The box!" shouted Harry, "Some form of force field!"

As the perception filter lifted, the group saw to their surprise that the bubble was actually camouflage and the white stallions were now standing in all their glory with magnificent illuminating golden horns on their foreheads and awe inspiring grand feathered wings.

"Flying unicorns!" gasped Jimmy.

They were brought back to reality when their attacker swooped high over their heads and hovered in front of the beaming sun, magnifying the glistening golden warrior. Before anyone had time to react the unidentified attacker forcefully dived down again, this time hitting Percy at full force in the face with a colossal golden mallet that sent Percy spinning through the air and crashing to the ground. The stroke Percy had been hit with was similar to that of a Polo player swinging his club. The two remaining youths looked up and saw a golden-coloured man with a unicorn horn and flapping feather wings on his back radiating shining light. He was holding a gigantic mallet in his right hand, had a silver belt around his waist and was wearing a helmet designed to fit snugly over his unicorn horn atop his head.

Harry raised his arms in anger and a bright stream of intense light flowed through him straight at the winged warrior. The guardian adjusted mid-flight but it was too late. He didn't have time to avoid the blast, but at the last second raised the mallet, absorbing the discharge.

Jimmy was frozen; he didn't react well to the battle situation. Aggressively Harry screamed to him, "Do something!! Attack it!"

That momentary loss of concentration was all the winged guardian needed. Raising the mallet in front of his head he thrust forward with all his might, flying directly through the beam, which was being continuously projected by Harry. The direction of the thrust and power deflected the stream of light straight back into the cloaked youth hitting him straight in the chest, making him instantly collapse to the floor. Harry was still conscious, but groaning on the ground with a burn mark smouldering on his chest.

The guardian landed elegantly in front of Jimmy gripping his golden mallet firmly with both hands.

"Demon, I am Aventiss, guardian of the unicorns, you will never take them. Leave this place now and take your fellow abominations with you!"

Aventiss pointed the head of the mallet at Jimmy, tightly gripping the handle with both hands. The horn on top of his head flashed, channelling energy down through his body and along his arms. A beam of intense light was forced through the mallet head, hitting Jimmy in the chest, punching him off his feet, through the air, and sending him crashing into the fence panel.

Unable to get up due to the severe pain Jimmy instinctively managed to focus, creating one last bolt of lightning in his palm, and threw it in the direction of Aventiss who was charging towards him with great haste. Aventiss merely batted the bolt away with his mallet and continued to approach, until Jimmy was within striking distance.

Aventiss raised the mighty mallet high above his head and was just about to strike the final blow when he heard the faint scuttle of movement behind him. Aventiss turned and reacted instantly to a second continuous blast from Harry who had managed to recover enough to go back on the offensive. Aventiss absorbed the blast and countered with a series of his own which Harry deflected with his hands. The battle intensified with strike after strike roaring down the face of the valley.

With blurred vision and dizziness, Jimmy raised his head and beyond the colossal struggle thrashing before him, an owl was perched on top of the wooden stable. The owl was seemingly enjoying the battle. *Is that Lyreco or one of the teachers in their form? Why don't they help us?* thought Jimmy.

Moments later the dizziness and fog lifted, however, not enough to really move or help Harry. Then, to his dismay he saw one of Aventiss's attacks break through Harry's defence, hitting him once again in the chest and sending him sprawling to the floor. Harry was on the ground again shaking in pain and smouldering from the strike.

"Nooo!" yelled Jimmy.

With a final push which might have been his last, Jimmy plunged forward with all his might in pure desperation and grabbed Aventiss's ankle. This was a weak attempt, but all the group had left.

The instant Jimmy touched the skin of Aventiss he felt a massive surge of dark energy pulsate through his body and out of his hands. Jimmy's eyes turned pure red and Aventiss immediately reacted by grabbing his head in sheer distress. To Jimmy it felt as though someone had forced open the door to his very soul. It was the same feeling he'd had when he grabbed the schoolyard bully Spike. In what felt like hours but was only seconds, Aventiss dropped his mallet and fell to his knees. He held his head, screaming. The fallen warrior kept shouting, "It's coming, the darkness is coming!"

Running quickly to the aid of his companions, Jimmy managed to rouse each one after their ordeal. Slowly struggling to their feet the children gawped in amazement in how Jimmy Threepwood had defeated the immense golden warrior with but a mere touch.

"What did you do?" said Harry with a clear stream of jealousy running through him.

"I don't know," said Jimmy. "I grabbed him to stop him hurting you and that happened ..."

Still holding her head, Talula applied pressure to her protruding bump and said, "Come on! Let's get out of here before that thing comes round and we're back to square one."

The group ran to the paddock storing the horses and as Jimmy grabbed one of their manes, he glanced over his shoulder to where the owl had been watching, but all he found was an empty spot.

Chapter 9

None of the group had ridden a normal horse before, never mind a flying one from myth and legend. Awkwardly, Percy struggled to climb on the beast's back and when he eventually did he completely lost his balance and fell straight off the other side, crashing to the ground. Dusting himself off he made a few more attempts and finally managed to climb onto the mystical creature's back.

Talula was a natural when it came to horse riding, leading the group in a gentle trot away from Puzzlewood Village. Of course the ride wasn't so easy for Percy.

Talula heard a great commotion at the rear of the party and gazing over her shoulder saw a cloud of dust being kicked into the air from the dehydrated track. The cloud tore apart and from within galloped Percy's horse, chewing up the ground as it sped swiftly past the group. The gentle afternoon breeze hurtled past Percy's face and he closed his eyes, trying to brace for an imminent impact. *WHOOSH!* Percy's stomach leapt into his throat and the feeling of weightlessness pinned him to his saddle. Forcing open his windswept eyes he grabbed hold of the reins until his hands turned white as a ghost's; he was flabbergasted to be soaring high above the clouds.

The awe-inspiring creature glided effortlessly, silently through the air like an eagle on a breezy autumn day. The stallion soared high in the heat of the air pockets before spiralling into a nose dive, almost as if it were showing off.

Against the wishes of its petrified rider, the graceful creature lowered its nose and flew back toward the populated village. Flying directly toward the top of a small wooden shack, Percy gritted his teeth in sheer fear and clenched the reins even tighter. Within inches of a spectacular collision the steed pulled up sharply and, whilst still gliding, galloped perfectly along the tops of the trees. It was a sight to behold and although it was the most exhilarating feeling Percy had ever had, he wanted to get off the horse as soon as possible.

The rest of the group didn't have such playful horses; they soon caught up with Percy and before long were flying in perfect symmetry as they headed back to the Elksidian Forest.

Shortly after arriving at the camp, Jimmy was quick to leave the celebrations and self-gratification and walked off on his own further into the wood. Throughout the return journey the guilt of injuring Spike, the school bully, and now Aventiss had ravaged his very soul. *I can't do this ... I'm ... I'm not cut .., this isn't me, I don't hurt people, I'm not gonna end this world, why me? Are they mad? I'm not going to do it!*

He sat with his back to the giant trunk of a fallen tree and sank his head into his lap. What would my friends think of me, what...what would my father think of me? A number of small tears trickled down his face, forming a puddle on the forest ground below. Around him he could hear the creatures and wild animals scratching and squawking in the trees, but he just ignored them. Looking down at the palms of his hands he saw the two unnatural weapons used to destroy the minds of two innocent, defenceless people.

Jimmy was getting more and more upset. *What have I done?* he thought as a knot formed in the pit of his stomach. *I'm not going to hurt anything else, I'm ...*

Then from the clearing where he had previously walked he heard the snap of twigs.

Turning sharply over his shoulder, ready to defend himself, he saw Talula walking along the path toward him. He quickly wiped away the tears, took a last sniff and sat up, not wanting to show any sign of weakness.

"We were worried about you Jimmy, are you okay? Are you hurt?" asked Talula.

Jimmy looked away and at the floor, "I'm, mm, okay, just resting."

Talula gave a caring smile, "Come on Jimmy, I can see that you aren't okay."

Jimmy looked at Talula, his eyes stinging and pink after the tears.

"I can't do this Talula, this isn't me, I won't hurt people, and I won't destroy anything else!"

"Come on Jimmy, we have no choice; this is what we are here for. You know what'll happen if you disobey Lyreco. You are nowhere near powerful enough to take him on, think about it!"

"No! I won't fight anyone; I am going, far from here. I will go home, see my father, friends, then I will leave forever!"

"Jimmy no! They will find you … but, but maybe it will be your only chance ..." paused Talula, turning away to hide a maniacal smile.

"It's too late for me," sobbed Jimmy, "Please buy me some time; tell them I am here practising or something?"

"Jimmy, how will you go? Where will you go?"

"Home," replied Jimmy, as he thought for a few seconds about his father.

Jimmy slowly morphed into the mythical Phoenix and a small flaming tear slipped from his eye, dropping to the floor and extinguishing in a puddle of tears. Jimmy flew off into the night sky.

A dark, soulless smile spread across Talula's face and she slowly walked back the way she had come with a confident snap of her robe. *That's him out of the way. I will tell Lyreco about this and he will be destroyed.*

Gently illuminating the night sky with his trail of fire Jimmy flew high above bridges, houses and schools. After an hour's flight he finally saw an aerial view of the very quiet, normal circular cul-de-sac next to the dull and boring Council Estate. Jimmy swooped down and smoothly landed next to the front gate after checking nobody was in the close or still awake. The instant his feet touched the hard concrete floor, a wave of exhaustion overwhelmed his weary body and he collapsed to the ground, returning to his human form. As Jimmy fell, he hit his head on the metal gate, and lay strewn across the floor, with no one to help as ruby red blood seeped onto the tarmac.

"My master," said Talula to Lyreco, who was admiring the beautiful stallions the group had returned with. Standing next to him was Xanadu, who snarled at the long haired girl.

"Jimmy Threepwood has abandoned us and returned to his father, I thought you should know."

"Hmm," the creature mused with an expression of sheer disappointment, "you have done well coming to me with this Talula, I thank you … now leave us!"

Glancing at Xanadu whilst scratching his bearded chin, Lyreco said, "This is the chance we have been waiting for. We shall destroy someone close to Jimmy, his anger will swell and he will be consumed by rage and revenge. This could be a decision by fate itself."

"Xanadu, go and summon the Gatekeeper, I have an important job for him to do."

Chapter 10

A blinding pain tore through Jimmy's head and, slowly opening his eyes, the bright bedroom light felt like a laser boring into his skull. The bump to his head was thumping.

Barely able to keep his eyes open, Jimmy felt his hair and clothes were soaked with sweat. A few moments passed and he started to find his bearings; Jimmy found he was engulfed with euphoria when he realised he was back at home, safe in his own bed.

His bedroom hadn't changed at all. It was still the grey, dull room it had always been, but he was happy to be back. Was it a dream? It was a bad dream if it was. Pulling himself up, he tore open the curtains and looked out of the window into the cul-de-sac. The world was normal again. Mrs. Fisher was pruning her roses, a ginger and white cat sat on an old rusted car parked near Jimmy's house, and dancing through the air was the sound of Mr. McDougal playing his Scottish bagpipes in the corner house.

Tilting his head he looked to the right, toward the Council Estate, and even that looked normal. In fact there were some new boys he had never seen, playing football on the grass in front of the large wall. He watched them kicking the ball against the wall for a few minutes before deciding he would speak to his parents to see if he could go out and join them.

As he turned, his heart sank and his whole world came crashing down around him. The black robe with the phoenix emblem was draped over the chair. Clawing at his sleeve he yanked it up and there it was, in all its glory, the number 6; the mark of Tyranacus burned into his skin. A veil of fear fell over his body and he ran down the stairs to see if his family were okay.

Sprinting along the hallway skidding through the kitchen and into the living room, he found his oversized mother still sitting in the same position, eating a slice of pizza with the box resting on her stomach.

"Mum you're okay? Where's Dad?"

Making no attempt to move, Marjorie diverted her eyes from the television and in a disapproving fashion replied, "Jimmy, you shouldn't be here. You must return to Lyreco or bad things will happen!"

As she said this she gave a mighty thrust forward to move from the chair, but she was well and truly stuck.

"You can stay to rest for a day or two, but then you can go back. We made a deal many years ago for you, and you will not ruin this for me!"

Completely shocked at the response, Jimmy's attention was drawn to the front window where his father was tending to the garden. Jimmy glanced at his mother, looked through the window and ran out of the back door to the garden.

Bill Threepwood heard the bouncing footsteps of Jimmy behind and his heart lit up. Turning he braced for the impact of Jimmy running at him for a well-deserved hug and they both collided in sheer joy.

"Jimmy, are you okay? We found you collapsed outside the gate, you have been asleep for days!"

"Dad, I can't go back, I can't do it, the things they made me do, I want to come back here, please, please don't make me go back!" he said frantically.

The feelings of happiness drifted from Bill immediately replaced by fear, sadness, and more so, dread. Bill looked away from Jimmy and in a quiet and solemn voice said,

"Jimmy you can't, you must go back. We have no choice. You cannot go against the wishes of these people; do you not know who they are?"

Tearful and overcome by anger, Jimmy replied, "Why, what is going on?"

Walking to a knee high wall Bill sat down, patting a space next to him for Jimmy to sit. Looking to the sky, with tears gently forming in his eyes, Bill inhaled a deep breath,

"Jimmy, eleven years ago your mother and I were so in love and things were so much better. Your mother was very caring, loving and active and all we wanted was a child to care for and to give them everything. When we heard the news that she was pregnant we were over the moon.

"We bought this house for more space, your room was painted all beautiful colours, with animal mobiles, toys, stuffed animals, and we were delighted. Then it happened. Your mother was about seven months pregnant, it was July and a glorious summer's day. We went out for the day about thirty miles away in the car and had a lovely time. We even planned how we would take you there to play on the beach, at the arcades and have chips in the evening.

"Just as we were leaving we felt a few drops of rain. We got back into the car and headed home. We were about five miles away when the storm just appeared. It was a bad storm, heavy rain, lightning, black clouds and … it was my fault, I should have taken more care … a car had slowed down in front of me but I didn't see it and we went straight into the back of it. Your mother was hurt; she hit her head on the dashboard and was rushed to hospital. She was unconscious for a number of hours when the doctors told me there was nothing else they could do, she was drifting away.

"After a few more hours strange things started happening. The machines started to beep gently and the lights flickered. The lights went off, then back on quickly and when I looked your mother was sat up, her eyes wide open. Your mother was mumbling about a bright white light when a dripping black hole seemed to form in the wall in front of her. From inside the hole came the worst noises I had ever heard. Pain, suffering, I can't even think about it …" he said as he turned his head, cringing.

"I looked to see if anyone else had seen this but the nurses just walked past. The hole grew and grew as a thick black tar splattered on the floor. This continued for a few more seconds and then a figure slowly emerged and stood before us. He was covered in a black ravaged cloak, carrying a scythe, and I saw all manner of vile, disgusting creatures and insects crawling underneath him. I also remember that all the flowers in the room seemed to just die and your mother's water slowly faded green, then brown. I don't know why I remember that part so vividly, it's just it happened in front of my eyes, I have never seen anything like it." Looking down Jimmy saw his father's hand trembling and he hadn't even noticed.

"The creature spoke in a deathly manner," said Bill Threepwood as he stared into space, reliving every feeling, every breath from that night.

"Marjorie Threepwood, your time on this world has come to an end. You will come with me now.

"In a deep trance, your mother pulled off the bed covers and turned sideways in the bed. I knew what was going to happen, I was overcome; I dived at the creature's feet pleading for him not to take her, not to take my wife and son. I said I would do anything. I remember the foul smelling insects started to crawl along my arms and my skin started disintegrating in front of me. My skin faded from blue to grey, and seemed to just wither and decay.

"Moments passed and a deathly chill filled the air; each breath burnt my lungs as it sent a thick, icy fog around the room. Your mother sat back down; the creature spoke again in a ghastly tone which I can still hear to this day,

"Bill Threepwood, you dare plead for the life of your wife with the Gatekeeper of life and death? Your son, Threepwood, has a future preordained!

"Marjorie snapped back to life, inhaling a long, deep breath like it was her first.

"I will spare the life of your wife for a trade. On the day of his eleventh birthday, I will collect your son and he will be trained to fulfil his destiny, he will become a powerful tyrant for darkness.

"I started to shake and looked at your mother. We knew it was a life or death decision and we simply didn't have a choice.

"The creature said, *I am glad you agree. Your life will be spared and I will collect him on his eleventh birthday. The boy cannot be loved and must be given a basic life with no friends, no attachments. He is to feel unloved and full of hatred. I will be watching from the other realm and will return if our agreement is not followed.*

"The creature then just melted into the wall, leaving behind a thick, black tar stain and the room instantly became warm, the flowers grew back and my arms returned to normal.

"I grabbed your mother and we just held each other until a doctor arrived. The doctors were amazed with the dramatic recovery of your mother, she didn't even have a scratch.

"A few months later you were born, but things were never the same again. Your mother could never bond or love you and drifted to a dark place, replacing love with food. Your mother is still in there somewhere, but so is the threat that if the deal was broken, he would return and take you both. That is why things have happened and that is why you must return to Lyreco."

Jimmy couldn't believe what he had heard; it all started to ring true. That's why she had never hugged him, that's why he was never allowed friends. It wasn't their fault, it was his destiny to have never been born or for this to have happened and he was ordained to fulfil what was written. Jimmy looked at his dad through different eyes.

"Jimmy, stay tonight to regain your strength, but you must return tomorrow, for all our sakes."

After spending a few hours with his family he finally agreed that it would be in the best interests of everyone that he return to Elksidian Forest the following morning. Sitting in his room for a few hours, Jimmy just stared into space, thinking about all that had gone on.

Chapter 11

From the window next to him came a faint *tap, tap, tap*. Jimmy turned his head toward the window but didn't think much of it, then *tap* again. Pulling back the curtains Jimmy was amazed to see a frantically flapping large black bat. Startled, he leant back, then realised it could only be Talula. He opened the window and in she flew, morphing into human form and gently landing on her feet.

Through sheer exhaustion, she slumped to the bed and sat down, panting heavily.

"Jimmy, I have come to warn you. The Gatekeeper is furious. You have broken his deal and he is somewhere here in this realm. He intends to kill your school friend Will Potts. He's going to make an example of you and will do it over the next few days!"

Frantically he replied, "No! Not Will, he's not involved!" *I need to stop him*, thought Jimmy.

"Thank you Talula, but how do you know this?"

"I overheard the Gatekeeper and Xanadu talking about it. He's really mad, you must find a way to stop him."

Jimmy sat thinking for a while.

"I need your help Talula, will you help me fight him?"

"Jimmy, no! It's suicide. You cannot seriously think you can beat the Gatekeeper of life and death?"

"I have to try Talula, people cannot die because of what I have done. Do you know when he is going to do this?"

Thinking for a few moments Talula replied, "He did say he would do it in school as a lesson to you. You need to warn him and get as far away as possible."

Jimmy's anxiety levels rose, "I won't run, we have learnt a great number of attacks and defences, I will be ready for him when he comes. Talula, you need to rest, I will prepare to go back to school and you will need to return to Lyreco to explain that I am coming back as soon as I can, but I must save my friend first."

Returning to his window he closed the curtain, just as he did he noticed an Owl sitting in a tree in the garden opposite. *Weird, is that the same ... Nah can't be.*

The following morning came quickly and Jimmy was up bright and early ready to return to school in order to save his best pal Will Potts from whatever was being sent after him. He was already dressed by the time Talula had opened her eyes.

His school uniform didn't quite fit him anymore as he had lost a little weight due to the meticulous trials and training. He paused and more questions flew into his already frantic mind. He didn't know why or what Lyreco was training him for. *What was the actual reason?* But at this moment he had much bigger concerns.

"Jimmy, are you really going to do this? You need to just run," said Talula, snapping him out of his daydream.

Turning with a defiant look Jimmy said, "I won't let them harm my friends because of my actions. I'll be ready for them!"

"You need to get back to Lyreco, explain that I will return to him, but for him to stop the Gatekeeper. You also need to look after yourself. You don't want Lyreco thinking you have run away too."

"You need to be careful, Jimmy; this is madness, but I think it's best I return to see if Lyreco can stop the Gatekeeper somehow. I will hurry back, be careful, Jimmy Threepwood. I hope you will be safe." Talula smiled, getting up from the bed. Her strength had returned from the last flight and she was ready to try the long and arduous passage back.

Opening the window the morning breeze and smell of a sublime autumn day flooded the room, tingling their senses. Talula climbed into the window frame, leaned out and jumped spectacularly into the morning air. Gliding for a microsecond as gravity forced her descent she morphed into the resplendent creature of the night and flew off toward the sun.

Glancing in the bedroom mirror, Jimmy straightened his red and navy school tie, tucked in his white shirt and put on his black jumper. He grabbed his old school bag, which was still full of his pens and books, and stuffed his robe inside. Checking the mirror one last time he told himself, *you can do this. You can beat this creature and save Will Potts*. This moment of pure inspiration was quickly followed by a solemn thought, *but I have no idea how*.

Jimmy walked the usual two miles to school alone as normal. He recalled how the crow and wasps had followed him months earlier and tried to work out how he was going to explain where he had been all this time.

Walking around the corner he saw it in the distance, Ravenshill Comprehensive School for boys and girls. Jimmy had never realised how awe-inspiring the school looked and was never so glad to be returning there. In the distance he could see the castle-like tower and stone wall all around the building and the famous Ravenshill crest of arms sat boldly above the entrance.

Underneath the crest hung the immense wooden castle doors, which historically must have been the entrance. The new entrance was now situated at the rear side of the wall through the large steel gates. However, to reach the school Jimmy would need to cross the bridge built over the River Bore, or as the locals called it the Bore River, and cross a main road with cars racing past at all times during the day and night. Before the bridge and main road, to Jimmy's left, was the school sports field which housed the cricket and football grounds, but to the right was a large boat shed, where the school stored all manner of canoes, boats and life vests. The school had a considerable area of land, but to get to any of the facilities involved the students crossing the road and walking a fair distance.

Walking into the school, Jimmy's mind was racing with paranoia that he was being stared at by everyone who saw him. He could also feel whispers on the morning air. Returning to the headmaster's office brought back the dire image of Spike's damaged mind, and along with it, Aventiss.

He was left sitting for a few minutes before he was summoned to see the headmaster, Bryan Ryding. Ryding was a tall, slender man, with prominent glasses, a sharp blue pin stripe suit, shiny brown shoes and a thin crop of strawberry blond hair on his head.

The headmaster's office was gleaming with smooth and varnished light brown oak, with a huge oak desk separating them both. Ryding spoke in a very posh and stiff upper lip accent.

"Ah Jimmy, I hope you enjoyed your last school, but I am glad you have come back and re-joined us."

Looking puzzled, Jimmy nodded, "Yes, urm, new school … and then I returned?"

"Don't worry Jimmy, your father dealt with it all and he has just phoned me again. You have been re-registered so off you go; I believe you have maths first thing."

Rising from the chair he looked at the overly smiling headmaster and turned to walk away. He opened the heavy oak door and glanced back one last time over his left shoulder to say goodbye. Out of the corner of his eye he was sure he saw the headmaster's eyes roll around in his sockets in a clockwise circle. *Couldn't have been.*

Jimmy ran as fast as he could to find Will Potts. Growing up he wasn't allowed any friends and for the reasons he now knew, he wasn't the most social or talkative person. Will was the best friend he had.

"Jimmy!" said Will, with an air of surprise and happiness at seeing his friend.

Will, although a generally normal boy, spent most of his time at home playing on the computer consoles his parents happily bought him; it was because of this that Will, like Jimmy, also didn't have many friends.

"Where have you been Jimmy? It's been months and the teachers just said you went to a different school. But I knew you wouldn't just go!"

Eagerly replying, Jimmy made himself sit next to his friend. "Will, I can't explain this but I have been away and things have happened. You … you are in danger, but I just can't go into it. You need to stay with me, I'll protect you!"

"You'll protect me, *puuhh* Jimmy Threepwood, protect me! Haha!"

Jimmy grabbed Will on the arm. His eyes darkened a fiery red and in a deep, dark and deathly voice he said,

"I'm not messing about Will, you are in real danger, and you will stay close to me!"

After their first lesson, both students went to the Chemistry Lab. Jimmy recalled that this was the classroom where the incident had happened only a few months ago. The accident was the start, the place where he received the mark of Tyranacus.

The students sat in their places with their books open, when to Jimmy's amazement, in walked Mr. Harry Tuft. Bumbling in, still in his silly raincoat and still mumbling to himself. Harry Tuft kept looking up at Jimmy, then carried on teaching the class periodically.

Harry Tuft showed the class how to create a potent pink potion using a white powder, a green leaf, and a hint of salt. He allowed all the class to create their own and when they were all ready, he shouted excitedly, "Students, drink, drink the potion; you will feel like you are on cloud nine!"

Trustingly and as requested all the students quickly drank the drink, all except for Jimmy. Within seconds the students started to gently rock their heads back and forth and in tandem rested their heads on the tables before them.

Fear struck Jimmy as he scrambled for his robe. "'*SSSS* have no fear, Threepwood, I will not harm you. I am here to help. Why did you run away Thhhreeepwood?"

Angrily Jimmy replied, "You know why I left, you are all evil and want me to do evil things. I will not do it!"

"Be careful Jimmy, your *parentssss* made a deal, if you do not return *sssomeone* will pay. Be careful!"

"Look, Iveco, I will return, I sent Talula to pass on the message that I will return, I-I-I just need to help my friend."

"We grow impatient, you *bessst* return with *hassste* before anything ... bad *happensss*."

Iveco and Idlewhich ripped out of their skin, discarded it on the classroom floor and disappeared into thin air. *Ding Ding Ding Ding* rang the school bell and instantly all the class woke up and rushed out of the classroom for lunch. No one even noticed the discarded rubber skin.

Jimmy was the last one to leave the classroom and glanced to see the synthetic rubber skin crumpled on the tiled floor. *I can't get distracted; this is the best time for the Gatekeeper to strike.*

Jimmy ate his school dinner with Will but he had so much on his mind that he barely noticed Spike, the school bully; slowly walking past him without speaking to anyone before sitting on his own toward the rear of the lunch hall. To his amazement, the other kids were turning and taunting Spike, throwing chips which just '*buffed*' off his head dropping onto the table and floor.

"What happened to Spike?"

Will smiled, "He's been like that since that day you pulled him off me. You were a hero, the end of the bully. Now he just ignores people, goes to his lessons, and goes home. I don't know what you did but he's a shell of his former self."

An air of guilt flooded over Jimmy; *I did that? I never meant to hurt him. I must find a way to stop this. If I can convince Talula, and then maybe Percy, we can end this...*

Chapter 12

The rest of the day and the first two lessons of the next day were completely uneventful. Will and Jimmy attended the PE lesson first thing, then French in the second lesson spot before lunch time.

They sat in their normal spot at lunch as Jimmy looked on, full of remorse at Spike's dramatic fall from grace.

"Jimmy?" asked Will, "do you think it's getting colder in here?"

"No, it feels normal. Look Will, I'm going to the toilets and then we'll see if we can play football with someone, deal?"

"Yeah, okay," replied Will. Jimmy got up and, with his mind drifting and completely forgetting he had to protect Will Potts, walked out of the room, along the corridor and into the lavatories.

Moments passed before he could hear the eruption of screams and shrieks echoing along the school corridors.

"Will!" shouted Jimmy as panic flooded his body.

Flowing with tenacity he ran, pushing through wave after wave of his fellow students who were frantic and screaming around him. Eventually forcing his way into the canteen area he saw the phantom menace, the Gatekeeper, dangling Will in the air by an invisible levitating grip. The abomination was slowly clenching his fist together, crushing the throat of the weak schoolboy.

"Nooo!" shouted Jimmy as he ran to the aid of his friend.

Whilst running he realised he didn't have his robe. *Is the robe the source of my power? I've never fought without it*, thought Jimmy.

Coming into the Gatekeeper's view the phantom clenched his second ravaged bony hand tightly, emitting a cyclone of wind and with that every door in the canteen slammed shut, trapping the other screaming students.

To emphasise his raw eternal power, he took a hold of the minds of all the other trapped students and against their wills dragged them sliding across the wooden floor and held them in a huge circle. Standing in the centre of the circle with Will Potts still being fiercely suspended by the invisible death grip stood the two combatants; both were ready for war.

Concentrating, Jimmy was quick to summon a bolt of lightning in his right hand, throwing it at the Gatekeeper whilst simultaneously creating one in his left hand.

Distracted, the Gatekeeper dropped Will and he fell crashing to the floor. In sheer distress he got up and scurried away to the safety of the crowd. The Gatekeeper effortlessly brushed aside the two bolts of lightning. In response he raised a grim pointed finger and from within the sleeve of his cloak, hanging on the thin lifeless arm, a flurry of all manner of decaying, vile creatures projected; the Gatekeeper hurled them straight at Jimmy.

There was no defence to this attack and the whirlwind of monstrous insects bit, scratched and clawed at Jimmy's face and body, continuously causing cuts, lacerations and tearing at his clothing. In excruciating pain Jimmy collapsed to the floor. Glancing up just long enough, he saw the Gatekeeper grab him with his crushing levitation and he was thrown shoulder first, slamming hard into the wall above the Drama room. Jimmy plummeted to the floor, wounded and unconscious, with fragments of plasterboard, brick and dust crashing on top of him.

Focusing his attention back to Will Potts, the Gatekeeper ghosted toward him. The fragments of rubble started to move and the resilient Jimmy jumped up with all of his strength and landed on the Gatekeeper's back. Pure anger channelled through his veins and his eyes glistened blood red as he sank his hands onto the Gatekeeper, as he had done on two previous occasions, waiting as his raw power sent the mythical creature insane … but nothing, nothing happened at all.

Flailing his ancient cloaked arms, the Gatekeeper rotated at immense speed, and Jimmy saw the horror on the faces of his fellow students who were being forced to watch the unearthly ordeal. Releasing his grip Jimmy was sent hurtling backwards; he landed on the floor, shattering the hard wooden flooring on impact. Instinctively Jimmy released a right and left hand lightning bolt which again were brushed away by the Gatekeeper. Jimmy lay weak and defenceless on the floor and at the mercy of the phantom that had the power of life or death within his fingertips. Instead of finishing Jimmy off, the creature let out an eerie, bone chilling chuckle through gritted shards of teeth before turning away and silently gliding past the horrified children, disappearing through a vivid purple light.

Will immediately ran to help Jimmy. As he grabbed him he was still trembling with fear.

"W-h-hat was that?! H-h-how did you do that?"

Looking at his school mates, they were still held in suspended animation. The school hall was severely damaged; there was a hole in the wall due to Jimmy's impact, one of the supporting pillars was completely obliterated due to a deflected lightning bolt, and most of the windows were smashed during the struggle.

The hall doors forcefully flew open with sheer magnitude of energy, taking the doors completely off their hinges. In walked the headmaster Mr. Ryding. He looked at Jimmy with concern on his face, raised both hands above his head and then *WHOOSH*. A flash of brilliant white light brought a warm feeling of euphoria to Jimmy and his peers. A happy memory from his past flashed into his mind; a feeling of peace.

Jimmy awoke expecting his fellow students to be screaming, traumatised, but they were walking around talking as normal and the hall was as good as new; no, better than new. Some of the students looked and pointed at Jimmy on the floor with all his cuts and shredded clothing. The headmaster grabbed Jimmy by the arm and quickly escorted him off towards the nurse's office.

"How did you do that? Who are you?" Jimmy shouted as Mr. Ryding's eyes rolled around their sockets like a broken pinball machine.

"Do not concern yourself with that yet Jimmy, you must get home as fast as you can, I fear you may have scared off the Gatekeeper from Potts, but your mother is very, very vulnerable!"

"No! Not my mother, they, they had a deal; he couldn't get Will, so he will go for her!" Jimmy realised in disbelief.

Running out of the entrance, Jimmy hurried around the corner, along the wall and jumped, morphing into the magical Phoenix. He flew home as fast as his wings would carry him, knowing that he would be weak when he arrived; but he didn't care, this was the fastest way.

The flight home seemed endless. Jimmy had a real concern for his mother and the story his father had told him rang through his mind.

Your mother was caring and loving; he will be unloved, no attachment, full of hatred.

It wasn't her fault; he had made her that way. He had ruined her life to get to me.

The anger pulsating through Jimmy made him stronger, more determined. Flying faster than he ever had before, he approached his home ... Then he saw them, two ambulances, police cars, police officers, lights, police tape. It all merged into a haze.

"Nnnnooooooo!!" He was too late.

Panicking, Jimmy dived toward the house, crashing unnoticed into the rear garden. Jimmy burst through the back door, and there was Marjorie Threepwood sitting in the chair in the living room. It took Jimmy a few seconds to register. He looked at his mother; she was crying, a police officer in front of her.

A solid knot formed painfully in the pit of his stomach. "DAD!"

He charged through the kitchen and straight through a police officer standing in his way, before running up the stairs and into the bedroom.

It hit Jimmy like he had just run into a brick wall; all he could do was collapse onto the floor. His father, his friend, the only person who had ever shown him compassion, shown him love, was lying motionless on the bed with a paramedic standing over him filling in paperwork.

"NOOOOOOOO!!!! Dad!" screamed Jimmy as he sprang to his feet and ran to the bed.

A police officer grabbed him and held him back "DADDD!!"

"Calm down, lad," said the Welsh officer, "let the paramedics do their job. They are doing all they can."

This was the moment Jimmy saw it, a look that would haunt him for the rest of his life. A solemn glance that burnt the image onto the very retinas of his eyes. The lone female paramedic shook her head, squeezed her lips together in sympathy. Jimmy knew it was the end. All he could do was fall to the floor with tears streaming down his face. He was now alone in the world.

Jimmy remained in that position for a few minutes when he heard the familiar sound of scratching from his bedroom window. At this desperate hour Jimmy needed someone, anyone, to hold. Running to his room he yanked the window open hoping, wishing to see Talula. To his dismay, in flew the black crow, which with a distortion of light transformed into Lyreco.

"Jimmy, I saw the lights and cars, I'm so sorry Jimmy; I came to help you as soon as I heard. What happened?"

"I don't-*sniff*- know yet-*sniff*- I've just got here."

"I'm sorry, Jimmy." Lyreco grabbed and hugged Jimmy who simply broke down on his shoulder. Looking beyond Jimmy out onto the landing a sinister grin appeared smoothly across Lyreco's face with a little sparkle glistening in his eye.

Gently pushing Jimmy away whilst firmly holding his shoulders and staring into his lost eyes, Lyreco said: "Jimmy, I came as soon as Talula told me. She is trying to get here too but needed to rest. You must stay here for a few days, I will return once you have spent time with your mother. Do not fear; your mother will be safe. I will take Xanadu to try and find the Gatekeeper." Lyreco paused. "Bill Threepwood will be avenged."

Eagerly Lyreco climbed back out of the window and, before Jimmy could blink, he was gone. The heartbroken child dropped back to the floor, crying into his knees.

Hours passed and slowly everyone left the house. The hardest part for Jimmy was seeing Bill Threepwood, his father, being carried out by the Grimey and Western Undertakers. They were all very nice and polite with Jimmy, but he was concerned they were both very old; in fact, he wasn't entirely sure they could manage to take his father without struggling or dropping him. However, they managed and the house fell silent.

As the undertakers were leaving the house they handed a small card to Jimmy's mother and he could hear the undertaker speak in the softest and most sincere voice possible. The conversation was clearly about the funeral arrangements; basic details of dates and times, venues and flowers. Marjorie was clearly upset, showing more compassion than Jimmy had ever seen in her before. She was devastated, but couldn't compile the words to reply. Bowing his head courteously the undertaker carefully positioned his black top hat on his head and it was over; they were gone. Mortified, Jimmy continued sitting on the floor; his world was empty, for the first time ever he felt truly alone.

Memories flashed through Jimmy's mind of his father's kindness and love, when he heard movement downstairs. The slow, methodical progress continued through the kitchen before the fifth and tenth, and top step gave their traditional yelp. Creaking, the bedroom door was apprehensively nudged open. Turning Jimmy saw his mother peering through the gap; she gave him a mournful smile when she saw him. Marjorie pushed the door and walked in.

The instant Jimmy saw her a flashback leapt across his mind. The words his father had told him danced before his eyes in bold italic letters. *Your mother was caring and loving*.

From the doorway Marjorie asked in a soft, affectionate voice,

"Are you okay? Do you want anything to eat?" Jimmy was surprised; she had never spoken to him like this before.

Listening, Jimmy could hear the soft rumble of sadness and regret in her voice. Smiling; he simply replied, "I'm fine thank you."

Marjorie gave a half smile, shut the door and walked back down stairs. Jimmy sat back and tried to remember a time in his life when she had been that nice to him. He couldn't think of one. He realised his mother's action wasn't the greatest show of affection, but it was a start.

A few hours passed when there was a knock on the door. There was no movement downstairs, so he got up, wiped his eyes and ran down the passage to open the front door. Standing in front of him was Will Potts. Will Potts ... Jimmy had forgotten about Will and the mammoth event that had taken place only a few hours earlier.

Will looked sheepishly at the floor and said, "Hi Jimmy, I heard about your dad, I'm, I'm sorry."

Will just stood there looking awkward; he didn't know whether to say more or be quiet. The silence continued for a few more seconds, but it seemed like hours to them both.

"Jimmy, I've brought your bag, you left it at the school before you ran off. Ryding tried to take it but I grabbed it and said I would return it ..." With a thankful smile Jimmy took the bag, placing it on the stairs behind him.

"Thank you Will, I need to be on my own right now but I will see you in school in a few days." Jimmy nodded in gratitude, closed the door and walked slowly back up the stairs.

Sitting on the edge of his bed Jimmy didn't have any tears left to cry. Pulling open the zipped, singed, dusty school bag the first thing he noticed was the black robe with the Phoenix symbol resting at the top, staring back at him. The more he looked at the robe, the angrier he became.

Lyreco, Talula, Percy, and Harry flashed fiercely through his mind, followed by the grotesque Xanadu and then the Gatekeeper, the abomination.

"The Gatekeeper did this! He will pay for what he has done to me!" muttered Jimmy furiously.

The anger boiled throughout his body, along his veins, and, closing his eyes, he felt the uncontrollable surge intensify. Jimmy opened his eyes and his hands were pulsating and surrounded by pure green fire. Previously it had been a normal yellow flame. Looking down he noticed that he was hovering above his bed and his whole body was radiating this green inferno. Jimmy was hovering and had the intensity of the Phoenix, but he was still in his normal human form.

With every thought of the Gatekeeper, the angrier he became. The anger was consuming Jimmy, he could no longer control it, it was radiating out of every pore in his body. He was getting hotter and hotter, then ... *Boom!*

The raw power blasted out of his body, impacting the wall with all Jimmy's intensity and fury. The house rattled, vibrated. The walls were dancing with green flames, the ceiling set alight, then it stopped and Jimmy fell to the floor exhausted. Marjorie bounded up the stairs as quickly as she could, saw the smoke and flames, grabbed the bed quilt and smothered the fire. Jimmy was on his knees with black smoke billowing off him. Marjorie dragged the quilt over him but after only a matter of seconds Jimmy's body heat burnt through the fabric and it crumbled to ash.

Marjorie stood back in amazement, watching to see what would happen next. Gradually, Jimmy slowly started to come round. Feeling weak and trembling throughout he struggled to his feet; Marjorie grabbed him to help, expecting him to still be white hot. In fact, he was the complete opposite, he was ice cold.

Marjorie saw his black robe on the floor. Bending down she picked it up and wrapped it around his shoulders to keep him warm, then hugged him until his colour returned. Jimmy was unable to move or respond but this was the first time he could ever remember being held in a loving fashion by his mother and it felt good. Jimmy asked, "Mum, what happened? How did he die?"

Marjorie, gently pushing Jimmy away, said, "I-I-I was in the living room and the hooded creature came in wearing a black cloak. He charged past me, went straight up the stairs and I heard your father scream, but by the time I got there the creature had gone and-and ..." she stopped to sniff, "your father ..." Tears streamed down their faces and they just held each other. That's all that they could do.

Five days had passed as Jimmy stared into the mirror straightening his white collar and black tie. He didn't know what to expect at a funeral. Feeling sad, he was unable to cry anymore. During the last few days Jimmy and his mother had grown close, closer than they had ever been. Once again he didn't want to go back to the other world but he knew he had to, no, needed to. He wanted the power with one specific aim … to destroy the Gatekeeper, and he knew Lyreco and the fellow teachers were the only ones who could help.

Outside the window the sound of cars pulling up and turning in the cul-de-sac screeched over the tarmac. Jimmy looked out of the window and saw the extended black funeral cars with their long glass windows. In the living room below, the family gathered and were talking to Marjorie Threepwood, but Jimmy still wanted to be alone; he didn't want people feeling sorry for him. One by one the family members left the house climbing into the back of the cars. Jimmy was the last to leave the house with his mother and they sat in the rear of the lead car. Although there was a clear atmosphere of sadness, the family in the cars were all glad to see each other and were talking about the past. It had been a long time since Jimmy had seen his family; some had never even met him.

The cars pulled up to a large house with a gold sign displayed on the entrance pillar, *Grimy and Western Undertakers*. Jimmy walked into the large house and what had originally been the living room was now an empty, yet grand area designed for the family members to congregate. The rumble of noise groaned above the crowd, and Jimmy stood at the entrance, greeting everyone who entered. After ten minutes the group were called into the main room, where the funeral would take place. The close family were asked to lead the way and sat in the first five rows. There was a large number of people attending and this, to Jimmy, highlighted the kind of person Bill Threepwood was; kind, gentle and loved.

The Vicar spoke some kind words and then identified the first song. Whilst singing, Jimmy felt a lump appear in the back of his throat and the hardest fight he ever had began; the fight to hold back the tears. Every time he thought about his dad he could feel the lump coming higher and higher up his throat and in the end he had to think of something, anything to keep his thoughts away. *I can't cry. I won't cry!* thought Jimmy, gritting his teeth, *I can't show any sign of weakness. I have to remain strong; it's the only way I can beat the Gatekeeper. I'm on my own now.*

After the service had taken place the family stepped outside into the most horrendous storm. There, Mr. Grimey asked Marjorie if they wanted to go straight to the burial or wait for the rain to stop. Marjorie asked a few of the guests but decided it was better to have it done and say her last goodbyes straight away. They drove to the site, but Jimmy was just too overwhelmed and decided to stand close enough to hear but far enough to be away from the crowd.

A short distance away, two unnoticed and lone figures sat restless on an old gravestone. Watching, Xanadu said to Lyreco, "Did you feel the power of the boy? When angry the boy's power intensifies tenfold."

Smiling, Lyreco replied, "Yes, his pure anger alone nearly tore the house down and he didn't even mean to do it, he is definitely one of the chosen four; in fact he could easily be the most powerful of them all."

With that he morphed into the crow and flew, landing on a branch above Jimmy's head as he watched the final stages of the funeral, standing, soaking wet in the rain.

Once the service was finally over and the cars started to disperse, Jimmy could once again feel the pure rage forming in his stomach. It was here that he heard the familiar squawk above him. Jimmy looked up and there was Lyreco, sitting on a branch with his legs dangling over the edge. Jumping down he landed on the soft, slushy earth below.

"This is a sad day Jimmy, but I can help you. I have been unable to locate the Gatekeeper, but I can help you harness that immense power of yours and one day you will have your revenge and destroy him, but only with my help. Will you return with me? Do you want the ultimate power?"

Jimmy looked at Lyreco, looked at the burial site, and saw the green flames flickering around his hands.

"Yes! I need to learn everything and I will avenge my father. The Gatekeeper will be no more!"

"Good, Jimmy; yes, the four of you will grow strong and as a group you will avenge the death of your father. Come to the Elksidian Forest tomorrow and your training will continue." Lyreco slowly disintegrated into thin air and with a crackle was gone. The instant Lyreco had gone, something bit into the back of Jimmy's mind. Something had just happened which sparked a memory, but he couldn't remember what?

Lyreco re-appeared back in the Elksidian Forest next to the centre flame. In front of him were his students, Talula, Harry and Percy. Giving a maniacal smile and in a victorious tone, he announced,

"My students, the deception has worked. Percy, your trick to distract Jimmy with the real Gatekeeper was perfect. The blame has been deflected onto him whilst painting us as Jimmy's saviours, and Talula … Talula - the outstanding disguise, no one would have guessed it was you in the black cloak walking into the Threepwood house and administering the deadly poison to poor, weak

Bill. What more can I say? Jimmy will rejoin us tomorrow, overcome by rage and fury, and will do whatever we require of him in order to achieve the ultimate power. You four will achieve the undisputed power and open the void to free Tyranacus and purge this world forever."

The three warriors raised their arms in victory and, in celebration, planned for the training to recommence.

Chapter 13

The following morning Jimmy was lying in his bed, staring up at the black, charcoaled wooden beams where part of his ceiling had once been. Jimmy was thinking about the incident in school, the damage to the house, but mostly about his guilt. Guilt at not being able to stop the Gatekeeper at the school, allowing him to escape, to come into this house; into his house as an intruder and, and … Well, to do what he did.

Waiting patiently, he was longing for his alarm clock to ring so he could get back to Elksidian Forest to recommence his training. As he waited there was a loud bang on the front door. The knocker pounded hard three times using the distinguished golden lion door knocker in the middle of the door. Rising from his bed, *knock, knock knock* rattled once again impatiently.

"Alright, alright. I'm coming!" shouted Jimmy as he pulled on his jumper.

The eager visitor released the knocker and decided that rasping the door would bring greater results. Jimmy grabbed the handle, gently turning it and just as the lock bar barely moved over the lock, in barged a rotund female, knocking Jimmy to the ground.

With a blur of her bright pink skirt, pink jacket and yellow handbag the middle aged female forced her giant hat through the door. Peering through her wavy golden blonde hair and past her small pointy nose, she grimaced at Jimmy, who was still lying on the floor. A high-pitched screechy voice leapt from her vocal cords,

"Boy! Stop sitting down, get up! My car is outside, collect my bag … chop chop!" she demanded, quickly clapping her hands and chasing after Jimmy to move.

Instantly the impatience in the woman grew and she proceeded to hit him on the shoulder with her handbag.

"Go boy, I don't have all day, off with you!" With that she flicked him a fifty pence piece and walked off.

Jimmy staggered out of the door, wondering what on earth had just happened. Beyond the gate was a skinny little taxi driver propping up a bright green suitcase.

"Al'rite mate, £6.50 for the trip!" the driver said in a southern London accent, holding his hand out, clearly expecting to be paid.

Luckily Jimmy had picked up his coat when he left. He scrabbled inside his pockets and found a £10 note and the 50p the eccentric woman had given him. Handing both to the taxi driver he snatched them, sat back into his taxi, pulled down the window and said;

"Al'rite mate, thanks for da tip, sees ya 'round!" With that the car turned and drove off.

Walking back into the house he found the woman sitting in the living room with a small rat-like white dog apparently named Penny, on her lap.

"Time for a cup of tea boy, off you go."

Approaching the woman the vicious little dog growled and tried to nip Jimmy's hand. Instinctively Jimmy jumped back, pulling his hand away when the woman, in a baby voice chuckled, "Good dog, nasty boy trying to get you, good boy."

Still nursing his hand Jimmy built up the courage to ask, "Excuse me ... who are you?"

"My boy, I am Aunty Maggie, do you not remember me? *Huuum* maybe you don't, I don't really remember you, anyway off with you, make my tea now and get me your mother!" she said, giving him a dismissive wave.

Jimmy ran frantically upstairs to wake his mother. Worriedly he pushed her door open; "Mum, Aunt Maggie is here? She has a suitcase; it looks like she is staying ..."

Marjorie opened her eyes and a wave of panic flooded over her face; she instantaneously jumped out of bed and started dragging on clothing whilst tidying her room.

"Jimmy, that's your Aunty, my sister Marilyn, but she calls herself Maggie. Go and make her comfortable, I'll be down in a minute."

Jimmy started to get anxious and thought to himself, *I need to be leaving soon, I'm gonna make this drink and go.*

Having made everyone a cup of tea he took one to his aunt, placing it on the table beside her. Letting go of the cup his reflexes were once more tested as the dog tried to nip him ... again.

Jimmy sat down and looked at the eccentric and colourful woman sitting next to him. Neither spoke and the atmosphere remained awkward. Moments later, in walked Aunt Maggie's younger sister and Jimmy's mother, Marjorie.

"Arrh Marjy, bad times these, I have decided I will come and stay a while with you. Now I won't take no for an answer. Wow, what's happened to you, it looks like you ate your other children! Hahaha!"

Maggie thrust a stern look at Jimmy and demanded,

"Boy, you take my case to my room and Marjy you come here and tell me what's happened."

Marjorie and Jimmy just looked at each other. The tragedy had brought them closer together, but things weren't completely right yet.

"Jimmy, do as your aunt asks, put them in the spare room, and then you need to get going to school."

Jimmy looked at his mother,

"Mum … I'm not returning to Ravenshill, I'm going back to the other school; I have urgent lessons to attend and there is something I need to do."

Aunt Maggie opened her mouth: "Not going to school? Going to another lesson, what are you talking about, boy? Take my case and go, I am here now. I am here for my little sister, you go and learn stuff!"

With an understanding grin Jimmy looked at his mother. "I need to do this, Mum; I will be back when I can."

It had been so long Marjorie Threepwood had forgotten how to love, how to show affection, and she simply grinned gently, nodded and whispered, "Be careful, Jimmy."

The last letter drifted from her lips when there was a heavy bump on the roof. Grabbing his aunt's case he quickly wheeled it through the kitchen, took it upstairs and went to investigate the noise.

Leaving the case at the top of the stairs he walked into his severely burnt and damaged bedroom. There, standing in the middle of his roof and peering in, was Talula. A smile beamed across Jimmy's face and as she jumped down he ran and hugged her, causing her to step back a few paces due to the sheer enthusiasm. Talula was the first to speak.

"I am sorry Jimmy, I was too slow getting to Lyreco and, and my information was wrong ... I'm so sorry."

"It's okay, Talula, I understand, you did all you could." Jimmy smiled, still hugging his friend for dear life.

"Jimmy we have to go to Elksidian Forest. The teachers are ready and we must get prepared and trained if we are to defeat the Gatekeeper. I have transport. Using our inner powers will take too much power and energy. We must be ready as soon as we get back to the forest."

Talula climbed out of the window, up the drain pipe and back onto the roof of the house. Grabbing his bag, Jimmy stuck his head out and the heat and morning breeze struck him gently in the face. He staggered out of the window and dragged himself onto the roof and there it was, the transport.

Jimmy expected some mighty bird, the flying unicorn, anything but a small, old rusted yellow Mini with one red driver's door.

"A Mini? What's that?" he asked.

Talula looked despondent. "What do you mean? That's my car, how else can we get back? You expecting a plane? A Tank?"

Jimmy replied, "No ... but a Mini?"

"Shut up, Jimmy, and get in!"

The car was parked on the roof, resting against the chimney. The height of the chimney blocked the bottom half of the car door and Jimmy, seeing that the window was missing, tried to climb through feet first. Jimmy was taller than the car was length ways, and pushing his body through he went in at such an angle that he was touching the driver's footrest with his feet. Pressing his foot to the floor, just in front of the driver's seat, there was a grinding crunch and Jimmy's feet went straight through the rusted floor and they were dangling, just close enough to touch the roof of the house.

Talula shouted straight away,

"Jimmy! Careful, this is a classic!!"

Jimmy pulled his feet out, shuffled back over the gear stick and sat in the passenger seat. Talula followed and sat in the driver's seat, adjusting the mirror.

"Why this?" replied Jimmy, "Why not the unicorns?"

Defensively and in an aggressive tone Talula replied, "Because I like this: anyway, it's been upgraded!"

"But you're too young for a licence? You can't drive?"

Looking Jimmy up and down and shaking her head, she said, "Jimmy, one day we will rule this world. You can throw lightning from your hand and we have pet unicorns, do you think this is a normal car? Have you not learnt yet? Put your belt on!"

Jimmy did as he was told and Talula began to speak, but this time not to Jimmy,

"Frank, we are ready, engine and perception filter on!"

In a flash, a yellow oozing, rubbery gel covered the exterior of the car and the engine roared into life. The engine sounded more like it belonged to Concord. With an almighty thrust the vehicle blasted straight upward with such force that it pushed Jimmy's cheeks in with the g-force, before the car nosedived, landing effortlessly and silently just outside of the cul-de-sac.

Once again the Mini raced off at great speed, dodging and weaving through both parked and moving cars. In the short distance traffic was built up due to a red light. The car maintained its speed, heading straight into the rear of the last stationary car, but as Jimmy closed his eyes for the impact the car leapt at the last minute, clearing the cars and the lights, landing a short distance away before careering off at great speed. Holding on for dear life Jimmy looked at Talula, who was sitting back in her seat, holding on to the door frame.

"Taaaaalulaaaa, who is driving?" Jimmy shouted, looking at the wheel which was turning and spinning on its own. Before Talula had time to respond the car thrust upward again, landing some distance ahead. Talula smiled, "This is Frank the Frog, the jumping, turbo Mini!"

"But it's a pile of junk … it's got holes …"

Instantly, as though the car was alive it slammed on the brakes, nearly throwing Jimmy out of the front window, and skidded half a circle to face the onward traffic. The passenger door flung open and the seat belt snaked open across Jimmy's chest.

"Wow, wow, wow!" said Talula, "Jimmy you had better apologise, or you're walking!"

Scared for his life and amazed at what he had just witnessed Jimmy replied,

"Sorry, sorry, I, I didn't mean it!" Instantly the car shot off, Jimmy's seatbelt dived back over him and clicked in place and they were once again jumping down the road.

Frank the Frog continued at great speed along the road, but of course the perception-filtered yellow gel made the car invisible to the naked eye. After a few moments Jimmy looked ahead and saw a lorry pull over just before a crossing area. As Frank the Frog approached it an old lady using a Zimmer frame stepped out into view. Jimmy knew there was no way the vehicle could stop.

"FRRRAAANK!"

Closing his eyes and waiting for impact he opened them long enough to see the car ghost through the old lady and carry on at speed. Turning over his shoulder he saw the old lady continue on but give a little shudder. She meandered on unharmed. *Ewww*; she thought, *draughty by there* and carried on as normal.

Frank the Frog left the busy areas and travelled along the quiet lanes into the famous docks area, heading straight for the sea. With a giant leap the car left the road, glided a great length and landed like a flat leaf into the sea; it was now full speed ahead driving on top of the water at a greater rate than he had experienced before. Talula looked at Jimmy.

"That's the fun bit done, gets a bit boring and straight from here!"

Jimmy, still shocked at what happened, thought, *fun, that wasn't fun, she could have told me about that*. Jimmy looked at Talula but she seemed deep in thought. Of course Jimmy was correct, Talula was thinking about how hard it was and would she be able to continue this charade. Percy was the one who came up with the idea to pass the blame to the Gatekeeper. However, it was she who walked through the Elksidian Forest to collect the ingredients to make the potent and untraceable potion, it was she who dressed up as the Gatekeeper and she who walked into the house, past Marjorie Threepweed who was petrified in her chair and administered the poison to the sleeping Bill, who had woken up screaming in pain.

What would happen if Jimmy found out? She didn't have a choice about the poison, she was made to do it. Although she had a heart of stone and no remorse at all, she had started to grow fond of the helpless Jimmy; but he was different now, far less vulnerable. Talula could see it in his eyes, he was driven by rage and vengeance and would have his revenge someday; it just depended on whom that was against. With that Talula drifted off to sleep in the front driver's seat of the Mini, with the car driving itself.

Chapter 14

Talula awoke and found herself in a dark yet familiar place. She had been awoken by a banging noise downstairs. Looking at the clock on the floor of her room it was 2:15 a.m. and the room was pitch black. She stayed there a short while and heard the recognisable sound of heavy boots trampling up the creaking stairs. She started as the door was forcefully swung open, crashing into the wall behind.

There stood a tall shadow of a man with black torn clothing, heavy boots; he was unshaven, dirty, unkempt. This man was Talula's father. Impatiently and aggressively he spoke with his commanding voice, "Lula: get up, time to go to work, hurry up!"

Jumping to attention Talula quickly scampered out of bed, dressing her small eight year old frame. Talula pulled on any clothing she could find and ran down the stairs where she met her father at the front door before they walked out into the night. Just before leaving, she glanced behind her at her kitchen and house and thought to herself *what a dump.*

Piles of dirty plates, pots, and pans covered the sink. Even the cat was eating some old food off of the saucepan, but Talula's father didn't care; he never cared. The estate they lived in was small, shaped like a half moon with houses on the outside of a large circle. The circle allowed cars to drive past all of the houses, and the circle itself was full of grass and used as a play area for the children.

The two figures wandered off like shadows in the night. Talula dared not ask where they were heading but she knew, this night like all the others, she would have an important job.

After about ten minutes they reached their destination; a factory warehouse. They both walked to the rear of the building and scaled a chain fence. As they landed on the other side they saw an open window about seven feet in the air. Talula jumped on her father's back like she had done so many times, ever since she could remember, and was pushed feet first through the window. As she slid through, her father gave her the final briefing. "Lula, take out the guard, and open the doors for me, quietly!"

Skilfully, soundlessly, Talula dropped to the floor inside the building and set about her task. Like a ghost she darted along the corridor until she found the unsuspecting, underpaid security guard snoozing in his office with his black and white television blaring in the background. Creeping up behind the guard she put her hand on his head and focused on her gift. The guard instinctively reacted, nearly falling backwards off his chair as his eyes snapped open. Before he could move any further he was fast asleep again without a care in the world.

Using her past experience Talula pressed the buttons on the control panel which turned off the CCTV cameras, and as she flicked the final switch the electronic shutters slowly ground open, revealing her grinning father holding a heavy-duty bag.

"Good work Lula, now help me carry these goods out, we'll get a fortune for this stuff. I knew that trick of yours would prove useful to me."

Eight years earlier Talula's father, Glen Airheart, had been a petty criminal. Shortly after Talula was born her mother ran off into the night, never to be seen again. One night, a few days later, Glen left the new born baby alone in the house whilst he went out to 'work'. He went to a small jewellery company, pulled a woollen mask over his face and used his crowbar to force open the rear door.

What Glen hadn't planned for was a silent alarm. Within minutes the building was surrounded and Police burst into the shop where Glen was arrested, looking at ten years for burglary.

As Glen was led out of the closed shop he opened his eyes and realised that time was becoming slower and slower until it had completely stopped. Everyone but Glen had frozen. From a wall to Glen's left sparked a bright light from which slithered a deathly black-cloaked figure. In sheer disbelief at the vision approaching him, Glen thought his end had come and death himself was coming to collect him. The ghastly figure stopped in front of him and, in a deep shrill that would send a shiver down the back of the bravest men, said,

"Airheart, mmmm, you have been caught stealing these petty items and you will spend the next nine years in a cell. That is, unless you take my deal ..."

Glen, with his hands still handcuffed behind his back and held by the frozen Police officer, asked,

"Deal, what kind of deal?"

The creature spoke again.

"Your daughter, the one who sleeps alone at your house, the one you have yet to name, she is very special to me. The deal, which I'm sure you will accept, is this; on her eleventh birthday I will arrive at your house and she will come with me; she will be taught power far outside anything you will ever see. In the meantime you need to continue as you are. She is to be unloved and not allowed friends or affection.

"In return, I will set you free from this … unfortunate situation, but also I will show you how to nurture your child and her … special power; the power to force people into a long, deep sleep which will also make them forget their last memory before they drifted off.

"I'm sure you can use this skill in your line of work. Remember, eleventh birthday, make sure she is ready, I will be watching."

Turning, the creature walked off into the bright light and was gone.

"Wait! What about these cuffs."

With that the handcuffs became loose and fell to the floor with a clatter. Glen ran outside, past the frozen Police Officers, and hid next to the wall out of view. Seconds later a flash of brilliant white light illuminated the night sky. The Police Officers all looked at each other, then one said, "Sarge, I've checked the building, there's no one here. Whoever they were, they're gone."

The Sergeant who had been holding Glen's arm was standing scratching his head. He knew something had happened, but couldn't work out what.

"Urm okay, if one of you stay to guard the door, the rest of you let's go, there's a shout at Oakhill Court, come on."

Glen smiled in a surprised yet victorious manner, and then went home to start his preparations.

Talula awoke startled and saw Jimmy leaning over her, giving a gentle prod to her arm.

"Talula, I think we have returned, there's Elksidian Forest, and that creepy castle in the distance."

Rubbing her eyes she leant forward and whispered something to the car's steering wheel. Instantly, the car leapt from the water, forcing Jimmy back into his seat and pinning him in place. The car glided in the air before landing on a beach area, bumping over stones and snapping branches before turning into an overdramatic sideways skid.

Both youths clambered out of the vehicle and as Jimmy stepped onto the golden sand his feet gently sank. Talula turned to the bonnet of the car, tapped it three times with her right index finger and whispered a strange language that Jimmy had never heard. Instantly there was a reaction. The car crushed and crumpled in on itself as though it was being placed in a large crushing machine and continued until it was the size of a small cube. The top of the cube flipped open, revealing a space inside and then out popped a small, green slimy frog, which stopped and looked at the two youths.

"*Ribbittt*," it said, and then jumped off into the undergrowth.

Jimmy looked at Talula.

"You didn't think the lessons stopped because you went away did you? Lesson one, conjuring—you'll catch up!" Talula walked off into the Forest and Jimmy gladly followed.

After a few hours' trek they arrived at the camp in time to see the others sitting on their trunks. The sun had gone down and the camp was starting to look darker and darker. Seeing the two return, Lyreco got up from his seat, walked to the fire and threw a pile of glittering silver dust into it. With a gentle crackle, the fiery yellow flame roared over the kindling, returning both heat and light to the area.

Lyreco walked toward the two youths.

"Jimmy, I am pleased that you have returned safely. Unfortunately still no news on the Gatekeeper, but I have spies everywhere, we will locate him and you will have your revenge. But first you need to develop your powers, and retrieve the Amulet of Trident. Then you will have taken the first great steps to achieving the ultimate power."

As Lyreco turned and walked away he smiled to himself. He knew the plan the fellow students had set for him had worked. Jimmy was more distant, he now knew the loss of a loved one, and he no longer seemed to be held back by any form of compassion or love. As Lyreco sat on the branch, Percy and Harry got up and walked over to greet their companions. Harry was first.

"Glad you're back Jimmy, you have missed some training, but I'm sure you will catch up!"

Jimmy nodded in appreciation. Percy then spoke,

"Sorry about what happened, Jimmy, but if we work together, we will have the combined power to destroy the Gatekeeper and he will be no more."

As both boys talked to Jimmy he started to notice something peculiar about them. He noticed that their skin tone seemed to almost be light blue. Jimmy also thought he noticed a very light aroma from the boys, but didn't think much more of it and put it down to the dark forest light.

The two boys continued talking to Talula whilst Jimmy walked slowly towards Lyreco.

"Master, may I ask you a question?"

Lyreco nodded, but didn't really seem to be paying attention.

"When I battled the Gatekeeper, when he was attacking the boy from school, I grabbed him. I grabbed him in the same way I grabbed Spike and Aventiss, but nothing happened? With them they were driven to madness, but with the creature ... nothing?"

Lyreco laughed,

"Jimmy, the Gatekeeper is no mortal being; he holds life and death in the palm of his hands. With but a click of his finger your friend and anyone else he wanted would have died on the spot. He is more powerful than you can imagine, and you will need to be even more powerful to beat him. The combined strength of you all isn't great enough to even hurt him, never mind destroy him...yet."

"But how did my headmaster get involved? When the Gatekeeper left, Mr. Ryding came in and somehow made everyone forget what they had seen?"

"Jimmy you are very special, you are by far the most powerful of the four and one day you will easily surpass even the Gatekeeper himself. We had to protect you. Iveco and Idlewhich watched over you as teachers and LaForte as the school nurse, but there are others. Mr. Ryding will also reveal himself one day to you as a teacher in this realm, but first you must attain that stage. You must next learn the power of conjuration, and then you must seek out and collect the Amulet of Trident. This will grant you access to open the sealed door to Sepura Castle and the centuries old power that lies within.

"Now go, speak to your companions, speak of how you fought the holder of life and death and survived; and tomorrow your training will continue."

Chapter 15

The following morning could not come quickly enough for Jimmy. He was ready, enthusiastic and almost demanding training. As soon as LaForte, the giant bold ogre appeared, Jimmy was there impatiently waiting to enhance his skills.

Once he arrived, the other group members joined Jimmy and kneeled on the forest ground in front of their teacher. In a deep and commanding voice LaForte started the lesson.

"Class, you have already started to learn the majestic and ancient language of the Elders, Mirosharr. This is the language of the dead and when certain commands are made, powerful allies will rise from beneath the earth and do your bidding. I have a deep knowledge of a number of these commands, but they are poor, weak creatures and can only be sustained for a limited period. You will need to study my commands and the Mirosharr language to control the living dead. However, it is foretold that the Elders placed detailed scrolls with all manner of demons and creatures within Sepura Castle, but of course this cannot be opened without the Amulet of Trident.

"Trident was the Lord Elder, creator of the current world, writer of the Mirosharr language. Sepura Castle was home to Trident and his eight Elders. Between them they wrote the rules on the current physics of the planet for mortal people, but also designed a way to keep this planet safe from the human race they created. They knew that every two millennia the human race would bring the planet to the brink of destruction. Therefore, they created Tyranacus, the Lord Demon, and encased him; sealed him in the centre of the world's core. The Demon cannot escape, but every two millennia four children would be born with the Mark of Tyranacus, '*6666*'. These children would need to be nurtured and trained until they were ready and of age. Then and only then would they have the energy required to break the Elders' seal and release Tyranacus to purge this world of all humans and return it to its original form.

"What follows is the start of the evolutionary cycle and the new world begins again. The period away from human contact allows the world to heal and repair itself. Two millennia ago warriors released Tyranacus but one turned on his companions and used his powers to try and destroy it. He was defeated and the purge took place as foretold. Tyranacus destroyed the warrior and once the purge was completed the Elders locked the powers away in Sepura Castle, broke up the Amulet of Trident and sent them to the sacred place where they would not be found until needed. The Elders combined their strength and returned Tyranacus to the core until the time arrived.

"Over the millennia the Elders grew old, leaving their human forms and living as spirits within Sepura Castle. That is, all except one; one was required to keep balance in this world. One remains to control the cycle of life and death and walks the earth taking and giving life. This creature you have already met. You are the warriors of Trident and will eventually release the mighty demon and help him destroy this world."

Jimmy was quick to ask a question. "Can the Elder, the Gatekeeper, be destroyed?"

"I feel your rage, Threepwood. Yes, when your training is complete and you have released Tyranacus, your combined power can destroy the Gatekeeper, and another Elder will take his place. But to achieve this, you must complete all of your training.

"Now class, you have learnt how to change living creatures into all manner of weapons and vehicles. This is very easy to do as the creatures are living, but their characteristics will still shine through. Harry, Jimmy has seen an example of a vehicle: show him a weapon."

Having a good look around the woodland Harry saw a rather large red and black spider scurrying across the dried, muddy floor. Bending down he scooped it in his palm and as he spoke, his words reverberated through the trees, shaking them.

"*Meeellllaaaatoooola.*"

Pushing through his closed hands a red handled sword grew in front of the group. Harry turned to the group, sword in hand, faced Percy and pointed the mystical weapon at him. With a mere thought, out of the end of the blade flew a sticky web that completely cocooned Jimmy, leaving only his head and face free. Harry turned and threw the sword into the air. In mid-flight he repeated the bizarre, ancient language and the sword transformed back into the spider, and, when it landed, quickly scampered off, terrified at what had just happened to it. Harry raised his hands at Percy, releasing a burning red light, which disintegrated the web and left him unharmed.

"Good," said LaForte, "This type of weapon or vehicle will be of great use to you in the future, I am sure."

"*Kaayyyylaaadie,*" commanded LaForte, causing the very ground to rupture. The earth imploded and a tiny, hand-sized red imp forced itself out from the ground. The demonic, winged creature scampered toward Talula and stood in front of her, frantically thrashing its razor sharp bladed claws at her face. Owing to the demon's pathetic size, Talula merely thrust her hand forward, pressing against the creature's head, and its miniature arms could do no more than thrash thin air. Moments passed and the imp ignited into a blaze of fire, then turned to ash and disappeared.

"The Imp, very weak but great as a distraction. Percy, prepare a weapon!"

Percy bent down and picked up a rather large brown cockroach with a glistening hard shell on its back.

"*Meeellllaaaatooooola!*" he shouted and the cockroach grew larger and into a shield which had the same shape, strength and pattern as the cockroach's shell.

LaForte shouted, "*Nyentooo!*"

Out of the ground appeared the human-sized toad warrior the group saw previously, still carrying a square red shield and a sword, wearing a Viking helmet and brown animal skin fur as a cloak. LaForte raised his finger at Percy and the Toad mindlessly charged at him and began thrashing his sword.

Percy parried the blows using the impenetrable shell of the cockroach. On the next blow Percy thrust the shield upward as the toad struck downward. The impact caused the sword to fling out of the toad warrior's hand. Percy instantly attacked with a spray of continuous fire, which forced the Toad to skid backwards as it managed to raise its own shield to protect itself.

The defensive gap created by the blast of fire allowed Percy time to concentrate before morphing into the monstrous blue and yellow dragon. The mighty dragon towered over the toad and without warning thrust his head forward, snapping his colossal teeth. The dragon would have eaten the top half of the toad, but rather than waste his effort, Percy just snapped together and the toad was gone, disappearing back to wherever it came from.

"Very good demonstration Percy," said LeForte as the boy slowly returned to his human form.

"You will have noticed that the toad warrior isn't that strong, but they never run away and will attack until they are destroyed or your conjuring power disappears. These are the two creatures I possess and they will assist in your journey.

"With time and practice you will master the power of conjuring and once you possess the Scrolls of the Elders you will have more powerful demons in your arsenal and may even be able to form a whole army.

"Now, group, practise this power whilst we prepare for your next task."

The group practised their new commands, Jimmy even more so than the others. With real ease Jimmy managed to create the red imp, but it was difficult to maintain concentration whilst thinking of other things at the same time.

Whilst completely concentrating and for no reason, out of the blue the thought hit him; the thing he couldn't quite put his finger on when he was at home. *If Lyreco had been in such a rush to save his father why didn't he just transport there? Why did he take the time to fly all that distance in the form of the crow?*

I know we haven't been taught how to transport, but Lyreco can; he has demonstrated it to us on a number of occasions. As Jimmy thought about it he started to get a wave of overwhelming sadness thinking about his father. As he was thinking he started to repeat the conjuring spell.

What Jimmy hadn't realised was that he was saying the chant over and over again, falling into a trance.

Suddenly from nowhere Talula fired a misdirected, bolt hitting him on the hand; he screamed in pain, tightly gripping his injury. At the exact time of impact Jimmy was in the process of conjuring a mystical creature. He fell to the floor and in sheer pain could feel something ripping out of his body. It felt like his whole soul was being torn from within him. He fought against it but a transparent phantom leapt from his body and disappeared. LaForte pulled Jimmy to his feet as he slowly came to.

"No magic should be able to harm any of you in this area! What happened, Jimmy?"

"I-I don't know!" replied Jimmy whilst holding the back of his head, trying to contain the sharp thumping headache which was hurting more than his stinging hand.

"Well you seem okay, go and walk it off …"

Jimmy staggered off from the group out of the camp and back along the path he had walked the night before. After a few minutes he saw a large crystal clear lake. With his head still cloudy he approached the lake and knelt before it. Jimmy's mirror image was reflecting in the lake from the morning sun. Scooping a palm full of water he drank it and felt its icy cold texture trickle down his throat. Still feeling slightly disorientated, he looked at the water again and this time shining back at him was his father's face.

"Dad: is that you?" asked Jimmy, reaching into the water. But when the water stilled again, the reflection was only that of Jimmy Threepwood. Giving a deep sigh, he whispered, "Don't worry father, I know what happened and you will be avenged."

Chapter 16

O ver the next few weeks the group continued their training and became very proficient at conjuring the ravaged bodies of the un-dead from beyond the grave. They also mastered the creation of weapons and conveyances from living specimens and learned the Mirosharr language. That was, however, until Lyreco appeared back at the camp and told the group that they were ready. They were ready to meet the perilous quest to Blackskull Mountain and locate the lost Amulet of Trident.

Lyreco explained that The Elders had taken the Amulet of Trident from the previous four warriors when their task was completed and returned it to a cave on the side of the hidden mountain. Once the Amulet was found once more and touched by the new chosen four children bearing the mark of Tyranacus, it would separate and reveal to them the wondrous powers within and grant them access to the hidden mysteries of Sepura Castle.

"My students, the path to the mountain will be treacherous and you will need to work together to survive. The cave is hidden within the mortal world of the humans, but even if they looked directly at the cave they would never know it was there.

"Also, I have noticed a change in the world.

"Somebody or something is out there, lurking in the shadows. Somebody doesn't want you to find the Amulet and they will do all they can to stop you. You must be ready at all times. You have completed the first stages of training, and this quest shall be the next.

"I have waited a long time for this moment, for you four bearing the mark to be born and have the power to purge this world.

"To find Blackskull Mountain you must be in possession of the Blood Map." Lyreco paused, looking at each of the children.

"The Blood Map is made from the pure blood of a vampire bat and solidified to create the texture of the chart. This and only this map will lead you to Blackskull Mountain. However, only one half was ever located.

"I mentioned to you the warrior who turned on his companions and tried to destroy Tyranacus. It was he who carried the map and he who ripped it in half and hid the second piece before he was destroyed. The Blood Map chooses its possessor, and will not be carried by just anyone."

Lyreco threw the half map high into the air and it slowly hovered on the gentle breeze back towards the ground. Just as it was about to rest softly on the floor the torn map flapped its end pieces like wings. It soared back into the air before nose-diving into the open hands of Jimmy Threepwood.

"Arrh Jimmy," said Lyreco, "you have been entrusted with a great honour: do not fail!"

Once Lyreco had said this to Jimmy he paused for a moment to reflect and then had the sinister thought that this scenario was following the same path as two millennia ago.

This is something that I will need to keep a very close eye on, a very close eye on indeed.

Still staring at the ancient, magical map, Jimmy felt its smooth, almost silky texture and wondered why it had chosen him.

Lyreco continued his story. "Through this time I have only managed to retrieve one half, and this half shows that as a group you need to travel past the Elksidian Forest, across the barren waste land, past the Lake of Healers, to the Arachnid Forest.

"Sadly the map is torn at this point and nothing further can be seen. However, after searching for centuries Xanadu has finally found the missing half of the Blood Map and it has been encased inside a rock situated in the middle of the Lake of Healers.

"I am not sure how it has been placed there or by whom, but you must travel to this location, retrieve the map, and then find the Amulet.

"I warn you, your flying unicorns are not yet ready to be with you all of the time, and the areas you are travelling to are not of human design or making. Any magic or powers used must be for destruction or defence only, do not use your inner creatures to travel. The energies in these mystical areas will force the creatures out of the spell and you will find a great fall greets you."

Jimmy listened intently whilst inadvertently rubbing his thumb over the shiny surface in his hands. He couldn't work out what Lyreco meant by *'not ready to be with us all of the time': what does that mean? He has also stopped us flying them lately. They are always locked in the stables and only tended to by the teachers.* As Lyreco continued to talk, Jimmy glanced around at his companions and as he did he noticed for the first time that Talula's skin had faded to a light blue colour like the others. Jimmy thought about it for a few moments and then, with a shrug of the shoulders, carried on listening to Lyreco. Once finished, Lyreco told the children to carry on practising for the remainder of the day; then they would prepare for the turbulent journey ahead.

The following morning at first light the group were up and ready. They had each packed a small bag containing food and water. The group left the safety of the camp and walked off through the treacherous Elksidian Forest in a direction no one had been for centuries.

After only a few minutes outside the camp, Harry was the first to speak.

"What's all this nonsense about? Turbulent, *puh*, it'll be easy! Get to the lake, smash the rock, pick up the map and walk to the cave!"

For once Jimmy was the first to reply. With a dark defiant voice that none of the group had heard from him before, he said, "Don't underestimate this journey, Harry, you saw what creatures live in our world, and we only just overcame Aventiss. Don't forget at one stage we were all defeated, including you. We survived by pure luck." The nature of his tone warned Harry and the others not to reply or challenge him.

Continuing along the path in silence, they had their long black robes wrapped tightly around their shivering bodies and their hoods pulled over their heads as they walked through the misty, cold, dark forest.

The full moon cast a silvery shadow throughout the trees. In the distance, covered in perfect white fury, the ever vigilant sentinel gazed down at their every move. After hiking for hours along a dusty, well-trodden track, concern rose within each of the group that the whole area was beginning to look the same. Percy was sure he had seen the brown oak tree with the scarred burnt trunk a number of times before. What also didn't help was the constant rustling high in the multitude of towering trees, and the sharp movement behind the undergrowth. The noises spooked the group, as did the sheer volume of piercing yellow eyes staring back from vast darkness and the sound of claws scraping along the brambles.

Although the passing hours had brought day light to the rest of the world, here in the forest it was still dark, with a thick shadow of fog restricting their vision and an icy chill sweeping through the valley of trees. Even with this going on the group weren't scared. They knew there was nothing in this forest that could match their power; in fact the group knew they could use the forest as a weapon against anything that dared to attack them.

After a few more hours of walking the children saw in the distance a small opening that appeared to lead into an area of bright sunlight and endless beautiful green and yellow coloured fields. Instantly the breeze and breath of warm fresh air rejuvenated them. The others had stopped to feel the new day, but Jimmy briskly walked on.

"Come on, we need to get this map and get this amulet before anyone else does."

The others looked at each other in amazement and sped behind him. Walking across the expansive open field, Percy was looking at the sheep and cows grazing on the lush green grass.

In the next field over was a beautiful white stallion. A stallion like the ones they had stolen from Puzzlewood. Percy thought back to that day and how the group were so easily defeated and how Jimmy had saved them with but a touch. But they were more powerful now that they had received additional and better training. *Arrr training,* thought Percy, *I could do with some practice, especially here with these open fields, no one will see me.*

Mischievously glancing over both shoulders he slowly held his hands together. A spark of light resonated within and he sent a fireball scorching towards a large oak tree positioned in the middle of the vast open field. The impact reverberated through the tree and it burst alight in an inferno of fire and fell, tumbling to the floor. A mushroom cloud of thick black smoke billowed in the air and from within rained down a shower of black and grey ash fragments which covered the group.

The others laughed at the carnage, and, holding their heads high with arms pushed straight out beside them, joyfully rotated in the snow-like fall. That was except Jimmy. He was entirely focused on the task at hand.

The group continued through the fields with Percy constantly practising his conjuring skills. Periodically he would focus and create a small red imp who would aimlessly run about looking for someone or something to attack. Moments later it would disappear. Percy then created the toad warrior using the Mirosharr chants. Whilst practising the chants Percy was almost licking his lips at the thought of finding more conjuring spells. As he was daydreaming, in the distance he saw smoke, and a tall-bricked chimney.

"There!" he shouted, "a small village; we can find some food and rest a while before we set off again." As his concentration dwindled from the tasks the Toad warrior instantly crawled back into the ground to where it had come from, as if it had never existed at all.

Chapter 17

The group walked briskly and in no time were standing at the entrance to a rather quaint little village. Just prior to the entrance was a yellow sign that read, *Welcome to Perrygrove. Please drive carefully* and two thirty mile an hour signs on either side of the road. Perrygrove was only a small village with a few houses and a variety of pleasant local shops.

The group lowered their hoods so as not to attract attention and walked through the centre on the main road of this quaint old village, looking at the furniture shops, fruit and vegetable stores, bakers, and a house with a gold placard outside which read *Old Police Station*.

Further along the road was a small post office and a butcher's shop where they could see the butcher chopping meat for the day. The people on the road were all glaring at the group as though they rarely had visitors, but none chose to speak and carried on walking by. On some occasions, they even picked up their pace.

The day had turned out to be fine, sunny and warm with not a cloud in the sky. As the group approached what could be considered the centre of the village, they noticed a tiny roundabout for vehicles and on the middle of this stood a tall, very old clock tower, which was no longer working.

The group approached and Talula started to feel a sharp throbbing pain in the front of her head. Harry also moaned, grabbed his head and said, "This clock tower,

I'm sure I have seen it before, I'm sure I've seen it in a dream?"

Percy looked at him and asked, "Well, Harry, what happened in the dream?"

Scrunching his face and searching his memories he replied, "I can't remember? There is something blocking it, I don't know what it is but I have a bad feeling about it …"

Jimmy walked around the side of the clock and saw a date had been originally engraved into the cold, dirty metal. Rubbing his hands to clean the indentation, he read aloud, *"Erected 1830 for our saviour, Lady Aurabella."*

Walking to the rear of the clock tower he saw that there was a statue carved into the back, which was approximately four foot in height, Jimmy guessed. The statue was of a woman in a long black gown with a cape. The arms reached upwards as though receiving applause from a crowd.

"That was Lady Aurabella," a creepy voice croaked from behind them, starling the group.

"It is said she brought peace to this village at a time of real austerity and cured all disease, making this a peaceful place to live and work. There are no records, just stories passed down over the centuries, and of course this tower." The man paused, smiling. "You four aren't from around here are you?"

"No," replied Jimmy, "we are travellers walking through but are in need of some food and a short rest. Is there anywhere you would recommend?"

The elderly gentlemen in front of them, who also happened to be the proprietor of the fruit and vegetable store opposite, stroked his long white beard.

"The Village Church is your best bet, just up ahead. I'm sure they may be able to give you food and shelter. If you ask they may even answer some questions about Lady Aurabella. That is of course, if you want to know."

With that the male turned and walked back to his shop and the group headed off to the church. As they walked away Harry turned back one last time. *I have definitely seen that clock and statue before, but where? When?*

The group continued and saw a church spire in the short distance ahead. They approached, hoping to find a kind soul to give them a place to rest and a little food. A rusted and fragile black gate held up a weak fence surrounding the church, its grounds and the adjacent graveyard.

Jimmy delicately pressed open the gate, resting it on a nearby headstone, and approached the alcove entrance to the church. With his arm stretched out ready to push the door and walk in, a weak, frail voice hollered from behind them: "I wouldn't go in there if I were you!"

The group turned and saw an old lady bent over at the waist, crippled with age, staggering towards them using a brown indented walking stick in her right hand. The old lady had been tending to an old grave, but was now slowly stumbling towards the group. She could barely walk. She was completely hunched over, wearing a knee length black dress and a black lace veil covering her face. Approaching the group she leaned in close to them and whispered, "I know who you are; I wouldn't go in there if I were you. You four are not welcome in a holy place, and who knows what will happen to you. Please come to my house instead. I will feed you and you may rest. I will tell you what I know about this village if you are interested …"

The group followed the old lady a short distance out of the village to a small wooden shack in the shadow of a black mountain. Jimmy felt a sense of unease tugging at his thoughts; *could they trust this woman?* Upon entering, the group were immediately hit with the foul smell of burnt flesh and death yanking at the back of their throats. Percy looked at Talula and pulled a sour face.

"Please sit, sit down, I will make you some food and drink!"

An hour went by and once the group had finished eating the old woman spoke.

"I have been waiting for you all. I knew one day you would come!"

"How would you know? What do you know?" snapped Harry.

The old woman smiled, "I can tell by the colour of your skin who you are, you are the chosen ones ..." reaching out aggressively she grabbed Harry's right arm and yanked up his sleeve, revealing the *6*.

"But how do you know?" asked Jimmy.

"I know a lot of things, I have been told to expect your visit, chosen ones, and I have been waiting. I know for example, a long time ago, that this small village was ravaged by savages constantly attacking it, stealing the food, burning the houses and livestock.

"It was also consumed by death and disease ... people, all the people were sick. Then, one day a saviour arrived. Aurabella. A powerful woman, she cured the sick, banished disease and ended the savage attacks. There is no record of how she did this, but the clock tower was created in her memory some years later. I know that you search for the Amulet of Trident."

The group looked in disbelief.

"I also know, but I bet none of you have noticed, that the raw evil power you possess is slowly decaying your flesh and one day it will rot away leaving you looking old, withered and with an even bluer complexion than you have now." A wicked smile grew on her face. "Or the evil magic may kill you completely. It depends if you find the flower. But fear not, I know all this truth because I am a direct line descendant of Lady Aurabella. She foretold that one day four young warriors would walk through here at the beginning of their journey, with signs of their slowly damaging skin clearly visible. For the more you use your powers, the quicker the onset of decay."

The old woman rose from her wooden stool and slowly walked to a cupboard. She swung open the wooden door, then impatiently slammed it shut before kneeling on the floor and ripping up a loose floor board. She pulled out an old oily rag and walked toward the four youths.

"My children, Lady Aurabella found these on her many travels; they are necklaces containing green Enoh stones."

Slowly she opened the cloth, revealing four perfectly cut, glowing green stones.

"If you wear the stones around your neck, they drain the excess decaying power from your bodies leaving you fresh, rejuvenated and looking young again."

The group looked at each other, with Talula quickly leaning forward and grabbing the green stone necklace and placing it around her neck. The others followed suit. Instantly the group began to feel different. They could feel the excess energy leaving their bodies and their skin returning to normal.

The group sat for hours, well into nightfall, listening to the stories of how Lady Aurabella cured the village, the surrounding fields, livestock and how she dealt with any intruders that tried to attack the village.

The group were starting to feel more and more tired. Then after one of the stories Harry asked, "How do you know so much; how was this passed down to you from so long ago?"

The old woman smiled, rose from her seat in a flash sending the chair she was sitting on skidding across the floor. Speaking, her voice became higher and higher, with her movement no longer slow and sluggish but rather eloquent and flowing. An aura of bright light slowly glistened all around her.

In a sinister voice, driving fear through the unsuspecting group, she shouted, "Because, my children ... I am LADY AURABELLA!"

Standing fully straight, her eyes started to glow wild yellow as she grew taller and hovered above the floor. Two mighty wings tore out of her back.

"I didn't save this wretched place to help these pathetic people. I saved it because I knew one day you would have to walk through this first town to get to the Blackskull Mountain, and you would know the location of the blood map ..."

Sizzling, sending the sweet smell of barbeque wafting around the shack, the flesh covering the old woman melted, dripping off her and leaving a vicious light blue hovering demon.

The creature had two horns on top of its head, wild yellow eyes, and sharp pointed teeth with razor sharp claws protruding from its fingers. The group tried to move from the chairs but their bodies felt heavy and lethargic, like stones. All they could do was move their eyes to look at the foul creature.

"Stupid children, it took me years to find those Enoh stones. They do not draw excess energy, they turn blood to stone, and after a few hours of keeping you occupied you can no longer move ..." The creature screeched a loud sinister laugh.

Jimmy managed to move his lips,

"What are you?"

"I am Aurabella, born over two millennia ago. Like you, I was sent with my companions with the Blood Map to find the Amulet and release Tyranacus. The world was destroyed in a flame of glory, but the Elders didn't grant us access to their power, they didn't make us Elders. We were simply cast away to die in the new world.

"For years I survived and helped these foolish humans to live and prosper, all in anticipation for this very moment. The moment I take the Blood Map, drain your power and command the beast Tyranacus myself!"

The creature gave out a piercing scream at the four defenceless children as the pungent fluid dripped off its teeth.

"If you do the bidding of the Elders, this is what you will eventually become. A long time ago we found a flower which rejuvenated our bodies, but after hundreds of years the black magic eats your body away beyond repair!"

The creature hovered around the old wooden shack, checked the windows, and then flew to Jimmy.

"Threepwood, I can feel great power in you. You will be my first victim ..."

The creature thrust out its mighty claws, which glistened in front of Jimmy and once again his face and soul felt like it was being sucked out of him. Jimmy was fighting with all his might but he could feel his soul being dragged further and further from his body.

Percy was trying desperately to lift his finger, and then, just at the last moment, he did it. It lifted just enough and he whispered with his last breath, "*Nyentoo, arrh Nyentoo!*"

Instantly, two toad warriors pushed out from the wooden floor. The first stabbed forward with its blade straight into the back of the unsuspecting demon, causing a shriek of pain. The demon turned hitting Jimmy in the face, causing him to fall backwards, crashing to the floor. The motion caused the green Enoh stone to fall off his neck, although Jimmy was still defenceless. He watched as the Toad warriors battled bravely, but they were easily destroyed by the demon. Jimmy could feel himself falling unconscious and, with a final push, he created a lightning bolt and sent it spinning across his body at the stool legs of Talula and Harry who were sitting next to him in a line. The chair legs disintegrated and all three children fell sideways, like dominos, onto the floor with the green stones falling from their necks. Jimmy was now unconscious after nearly having his soul sucked out of him, but movement quickly returned to the others.

Lady Aurabella finished off the second warrior and turned in dismay to find the group had been freed. Harry was the first on the offensive, firing a beam of continuous red light. Aurabella caught the beam and held it in the palm of her hands. Percy then stepped forward and unleashed fire at the creature who managed to pull one hand away from the beam and stop the fire with the other hand.

The two attacks were slowly taking their toll on Lady Aurabella, but also on the two boys. Talula stood behind them both and shouted, "One, two, three!"

In tandem the boys stopped their attacks and ducked as Talula unleashed a series of right and left hand fire bolts at the creature. Lady Aurabella, already weakened by the original attacks, knocked away the first three bolts but was hit in the chest by the fourth and fifth, knocking her to the ground.

Lady Aurabella hissed and snarled through her teeth as she hit the wooden floor. Green blood was dripping out of the injury on her back from the toad warrior and cuts from the bolts.

Like the wind, Lady Aurabella got up and was flying through the air as she slashed, catching Talula across the face with the nails on her right claw. Talula screeched in pain, but what Lady Aurabella hadn't factored in her haste for revenge was that in diving for Talula, she was now hovering defencelessly above the still crouching Harry and Percy. Both let loose with their fire at the same time, pinning the foul demon creature to the ceiling of the shack. The creature was shrieking in pain but managing to absorb most of the attacks even with both boys concentrating their fire.

Talula got up off her knees, looked at the creature and once again sent a barrage of green fireballs. Those, coupled with the concentrated fire, lasted only a few more minutes before Lady Aurabella set alight into a spectacular blue flame and the burnt ash rained gently to the floor. As the flakes of dust floated to the ground a golden ring plummeted from the burning remains, bouncing on the wooden floor and rolling as it hit the wall.

The group stopped their attack and ran to the aid of Jimmy, who was still unconscious. Talula grabbed him and Jimmy slowly began to come around; gingerly he sat up with Talula's arms still keeping him steady. Wiping the cobwebs from his mind he looked around through blurred vision. He could feel his body tingle as it repaired itself after Lady Aurabella's horrible attempt at taking his soul.

"What happened?" asked Jimmy, holding his head.

The group all collapsed onto the hard wooden floor in exhaustion.

"I thought that was it again! What was that thing?" asked Percy.

"That must have been the thing Lyreco was talking about, the thing trying to stop us ..." said Talula.

"Well, it's gone now, we need to move in case there are more things like her out there ..." commanded Harry.

"Wait," said Jimmy. "What's that?" He pointed at a key hanging on a piece of string on the wall.

"The handles in the shape of a 6." Harry walked and picked up the key before turning to them excitedly.

"I have seen this, this was in my dream; I know where this goes, COME ON!"

Talula had heard the golden ring fall from the remains of Lady Aurabella and as they left the shack she bent down and scooped it up. Staring at it as it sat in the palm of her hand the colour gradually withered away, leaving the ring a dirty green colour. Rubbing her finger over the rough surface she saw a name engraved in the centre, *Child of Tyranacus – Aurabella.*

This ring must have been attached to her life force somehow, I will show this to Lyreco when we get back.

Harry, followed by the group, ran out of the house, down the lane and back to the clock tower.

"Look!" Harry said, "the handle has a large six on the end like our wrists but the head is in the shape of an eight." Pushing the key into the *8* in the *Erected 1830 for our saviour, Lady Aurabella* sign, he turned the key as the barrel clicked.

Instantly a light illuminated from within the wall and the statue above slowly moved with the sound of scraping stone. The eyes of the statue turned yellow and the arms, head and body turned, focusing on Harry, who was still clutching the key.

"Who dares open the vault of Lady Aurabella?"

"Aurabella is dead; we have defeated her, open the vault or we'll smash it open, taking you with it!" commanded Harry.

There was a brief pause.

"I was created and given life by Aurabella to protect her precious items. Prove to me that she is dead like you claim."

Percy, Harry and Jimmy looked at each other until they heard Talula rummage through her pockets behind them. Pushing past the boys she thrust the faded, lifeless ring into the air.

"Here is your proof. Lady Aurabella's ring."

The enchanted statue scrutinised the ring and saw the markings in the middle and that the life colour had drained away. Having seen the evidence the statue closed its eyes, trying to feel her master's presence. Unable to feel Lady Aurabella's life force the statue had no further reason to exist. With a crunch, a crack split through her middle. The statue crumbled into dust and floated off in the breeze.

The solid clock tower structure scraped open on its ancient rusty hinges, revealing a cold, cobweb covered, stone staircase spiralling downward into a void of darkness.

"Where did you get that ring?" asked Percy.

Talula smiled, "It fell from Lady Aurabella's body during the battle and I picked it up. It has her name in it. This must be something the previous four children were given. We will need to ask Lyreco about it … but first, let's see what's down there." With that, Talula stepped into the darkness.

Chapter 18

Brushing through the sticky, moist cobweb covering the entrance Jimmy took the lead. Once he pulled the silky substance from his mouth and face he ignited his right arm with the pure green flame, which illuminated the tomb and allowed the group to walk down the spiralled staircase into the clear unknown.

Having taken only five steps a wild draught of air whistled past the group, nearly extinguishing Jimmy's flame as it flickered wildly. With a loud scraping of stone the entrance closed and they were sealed in with whatever awaited them.

Each spiralling step was made of solid, thick, cold stone and every footstep echoed throughout the crypt. There were no railings to hold, just the edge of the wall to press their hands firmly onto to hold their balance. Facing almost sideways, pushing against the wall, each of them felt for the next step by slowly and tentatively touching the ground with their leading foot.

The group were a little apprehensive as they continued to descend. After a few more paces the downward staircase revolved even sharper with the inside of each stone slab now barely half the size of one of Talula's feet. This forced the group to proceed with caution and to step only on the thicker outer edge of the step, whilst trying to maintain their balance. Poor lighting and the fact they could barely see their feet intensified the challenge.

They continued walking down and down until eventually they saw the flicker of a flame in a room at the bottom. Stepping off the last step the group walked into a large, open space with a stone tiled floor, each slab cracked, dusty and faded through time. Four flames intensely blazed in each corner. Percy marvelled as the flame flickered around the room, but more importantly danced off the reflective surfaces of treasure collected over a thousand years. Percy approached the tantalising coins, plates, statues and even old paintings that had been lost for centuries.

However, it was Talula who spotted the main treasure. Right in the middle of the room with gold scattered all around it was a large wooden stand, with a glass case on top. Blowing a thick layer of dust into the air, Talula rubbed her hands on the glass, wiping away the last remaining particles. There, in all its glory a hand written book sat open, revealing two pages. They were in awe of the marvellous detailed drawings and colours that had somehow managed to stay untarnished by time.

Talula opened the glass case and gently lifted the book. The book was very old and the spine seemed to just give way and crack under the small amount of pressure from her fingers. It was clear to Talula and the others that this book had not been looked at or touched in centuries. It was open on the centre pages and on closer inspection the writing was in black ink and looked as though it had been written with a quill, using a very old style of writing. The book was entitled,

The Forgotten Past. The Diary of Eunice Aurabella.

Talula read out the page.

"There were four of us chosen and taken away from our parents. We were told about the Amulet of Trident and the colossal power we would achieve. Three of us could not wait to get started, the thought of the ultimate

power releasing the raw energy of Tyranacus was exhilarating; but one of us was very different.

"From the start Argon Monteith seemed to be kinder; he cared about people, his family, the three of us and after a while he started to have an impact on the way we thought. It was clear he had an element of good about him, but we used that to our advantage.

"The whole group changed the day of the reckoning, the day Tyranacus was released as foretold. Argon did his part in the ritual, but he double-crossed us. Unbeknown to us Argon had created a small army named the Light Dwellers to stop us and Tyranacus from ending the world.

"He had found a group of warriors with special talents and hidden powers, similar to ours, and trained them to use their magic for good. A battle took place and Argon was destroyed; the others fled and were never seen again. I do think Argon won a place somewhere in my heart and he was sorely missed, he was a good friend.

"We, the remaining three, were then cast away to live in this mortal world. The Elders turned us away when the world was destroyed and we were forced to go our own ways and survive ...

"The rest of the pages are severely damaged but I can just about make out that it talks about getting revenge, helping this town and the plan to capture us and the Amulet of Trident to destroy the Elders ..." continued Talula, still admiring the detail.

As Talula put the book gently back in the case a lone page glided to the ground. Harry was first to grab it whilst still in flight.

"Hey, this looks like the pages LaForte had. It says NightStalker, and it's in the Mirosharr language. This is one of the scrolls. Aurabella must have kept it all this time. We need to keep moving but we should take this, I'm sure it will come in useful to us. Percy, Jimmy, grab a handful of that gold too, you never know what people will sell for gold." Full of excitement and greed Percy ran to the pile of precious artefacts and starting stuffing as much of it into his pockets as he could. He was still there as he heard his three companions climb the steps. As they left, one by one the flames in the corners blew out, casting the room into darkness. Percy was all alone. Feeling a little scared, he grabbed another handful of treasure and ran up the steps.

Eager to carry on their journey, the group scaled the stairs.

"Hey! Wait for me!" Percy's voice echoed from behind them, followed by the sound of twenty golden coins bouncing down the stairs. "No!" screamed Percy as he paused, before deciding he didn't want to go back into that room to find them.

Reaching the top of the spiralling staircase they forced open the weighty, solid stone entrance locked by the statue and carried on through the town on their journey.

The group continued walking along a long and winding dusty path, discussing the events that had unfolded and how they had been so easily manipulated by the old woman. They now had a fast realisation that Lyreco had been right and unknown dangers did lie ahead on this path. They would never trust a stranger so easily again.

Chapter 19

The group followed the half torn Blood Map for days with Jimmy leading the way. Somehow, mysteriously, Jimmy had forged a bond with the cloth. It had attached itself to him and felt as though it was feeding off his thoughts, his history.

The group had stopped at various locations along their journey and had spoken to a number of people, but none knew the location of the Lake of Healers. Some mentioned a lake in the distance, but each gave it a different name. What was clear was that although the map was very old, it had somehow managed to keep updated, almost as though by magic. Each town was in the location it was supposed to be, also each monument, regardless of how recently it was built.

The group didn't waste time during their expansive journey. As they walked they expressed their magic, creating imps, toads, firing fireballs and even using their inner powers to travel short distances. At first they were cautious after the words of Lyreco, but after a while nothing happened to them and they grew more and more confident.

During the nights the group stopped and set up camp in safe locations, creating small campfires and talking into the morning. When it was time to sleep, they all took turns to keep guard. On two occasions, when it was Talula's turn, Jimmy would wake up half way through and spend time talking with her, keeping her company and discussing her upbringing and past. On both occasions Jimmy had taken off his robe and draped it over her shoulders. In Jimmy's eyes it was a gesture of good will, the gentlemanly thing to do, but Talula gradually began to read more into the act of kindness and slowly, over time, started to listen to his words more carefully, on a few occasions adding more meaning to them than was perhaps intended. What was clear during their conversations was they knew very little about the pasts of Percy or Harry, but they knew, having been through what they had together; they trusted them with their lives.

After days and days of walking the group finally saw the extraordinary, picturesque sight of the Lake of Healers in the distance. It was a spectacular view with the light of the lake glistening from the rays of the morning sun, bouncing off the still sheet of blue. Prior to the lake were acres and acres of luscious green fields with roaming cattle, horses and birds gliding gently in the air.

Jimmy stared at the spectacular, awe inspiring view but suddenly had the sinking feeling in his stomach that when the time was deemed to be ready, they would destroy all of this, everything; nothing would remain. *Views like this will be wiped from the world only to be seen years and years in the future. Why are we doing this? Who says we have to destroy this world? I wonder why Argon turned on his companions, why did he set the mighty demon free if he wanted to save the world? Surely someone must have the answers?*

Harry looked at Jimmy who was engrossed in his own thoughts.

"Come on, we have a mission to do, let's get this other half of the map and get back!"

Jimmy shook his head; *of course, the map. The quicker I get that, the quicker we get back and I will get my revenge on the Gatekeeper for what he did to my father.*

The group made great haste over the fields and as Jimmy approached the edge of the lake he felt a double presence. Firstly he could feel the desire of the Blood Map trying to pull free from its resting place and reunite with its twin brother. He also felt the strong presence of another.

Jimmy's eyes darted all around the area, but there was nothing. He couldn't see anyone, but he had a creepy feeling that someone was watching them.

"So," said Harry. "How are we going to get to that?" he asked, pointing in the distance to a small island right in the middle of the lake.

In the centre of the island stood a rock the height and size of a small human with a golden placard gleaming in the morning sun. Percy, with his new found urgency, pushed past the others.

"Out of the way, I'm just going to fly there and blast the stupid rock with fire!"

"Percy, Lyreco told us not to do that here ..." reasoned Talula.

"Rubbish!" he replied, "we have all been flying during our journey and nothing's happened to us."

Without another word Percy spread out his arms as if expanding his wings and instantly transformed into the perfect yellow and blue dragon. Flapping his monstrous wings he lifted off effortlessly into the air.

Flying forward Percy was soaring over the beginning of the lake when he passed through an invisible layer of thick, wobbly jelly. In an instant he knew something was wrong. His wings and eyes became heavy, he could no longer flap and as he forced open his eyes he realised he was morphing back to human form.

Without the capacity to fly, Percy started to plummet sharply towards the water. Percy's eyes were now closed due to the invisible force pulling them shut. The others watched in sheer disbelief. From their vantage point they saw Percy fly above the water's edge and change back to human form in mid-flight. Percy was now hurtling at great speed towards the lake and then … *SPLASH!* Percy was in the water, leaving the others unsure about how badly he was injured. Whilst he was falling Jimmy tried to react by flying after him, but it had all happened too quickly, in the blink of an eye.

Without thinking Harry rushed into the water, pushing his way through the still lagoon towards where Percy had landed. Talula was also waist high in the water a short distance behind Harry, frantically wading through the lake when she felt something push past her. Turning, following the ripples, she saw eyes staring back at her from under the water. Talula picked up the pace and grabbed Harry's sleeve. As Harry turned to see what was going on something from within the water gave them both a mighty shove, pushing them backwards, high out of the water, causing them to land on the grassy bank.

In the distance Percy had also been thrown from the water landing unconscious on the small island next to the rock. Talula and Harry quickly regained their composure and pulled themselves up.

Determined they approached the water again but were quickly halted when a human form emerged from within, standing on top of the water, viciously glaring at them. The organism was in the form of a human male but was made purely of water, snarling at them both through its translucent sabre tooth fangs.

In an instant the organism glided across the water leaving a jet stream in his wake. Approaching at speed the creature thrust both arms forward, hitting Harry clean from the edge of the water; he landed ten feet away with a crash as he hit the grass bank. Simultaneously, a second organism appeared and dragged Talula under the water by her feet. Holding her for only a few seconds it then also fired her a great height out of the water. The instant Talula landed, three, four, five, ten, twenty more of the human shaped organisms merged from the water and swiftly skimmed across the top toward the fallen group.

Just short of the land the riot of organisms sharply skidded, sending a tidal wave of water, drenching the three magical youths. In pure anger Harry raised his soaked arm and let loose his continuous beam at the organisms. The closest organism merely altered its form, bending away from the blast and melted with a splash out of view.

Jimmy knew it was pointless trying to fight the organisms within the water, quickly realising that they were the water. The idea came to Jimmy to throw a lightning bolt at the rock to try and break it open. Gathering his composure he focused and threw a bolt with all his might, but it landed just short, hitting the island and just missing Percy who was still unconscious on the ground.

Then the next idea flashed into his mind. Once again he would throw the next lightning bolt in a similar fashion but this time aiming for his injured teammate. Whilst creating the bolt he intentionally made it slightly weaker so as not to cause injury.

This time his aim was perfect and the bolt hit Percy on the arm and gave him a delicate shock, which brought him straight out of his unconscious state. Percy sat up, looking around to see what had happened.

The lake creatures turned and, seeing that Percy was awake and sitting near the rock they were frantically and aggressively guarding, turned and glided at full speed toward him to save the rock and precious map secured within.

Now was the time for the second part of Jimmy's plan.

Jimmy created a second and third more powerful bolt and threw them one after the other into the centre of the lake. The instant the charged lightning bolt touched the surface, an electric charge streamed through the water like a thousand coiled yellow snakes, dazzling and sizzling with each drop.

The organisms' bodies, ravaged by electronic pulses, stood firm in their last positions violently shaking before slowly draining back into the water.

"Quick!! Percy, smash the rock before they come back!" shouted Jimmy.

Still a little dazed Percy managed to turn and unleash a stream of white hot fire at the rock until a series of cracks started to form. Instantly the rock exploded in a tower of black smoke and from within launched a yellow, ancient piece of paper projected high into the air, attracted to Jimmy like a homing missile.

The map hit the unsuspecting Jimmy in the chest, knocking him to the floor.

Percy, still on the island, didn't dare step into the still frazzling waters. Taking a chance that it was the water that drained his Dragon power he quickly changed again. Flapping frantically he flew high into the air, heading for land as fast as he could.

As he landed the group once again collapsed to the floor of the grassy bank onto their backs looking at each other; they were all battered, bruised and exhausted.

"Is this really worth it?" said Harry.

Percy was still dazed, having fallen from a great height, almost drowning in the lake, being thrown through the air and nearly electrocuted by his companion; "Great ..." said Percy. "Totally worth it," he confirmed as he put his head back into the dirt to rest.

There was no real time to rest or celebrate their victory.

Moments later the sizzling stopped in the lake and instantly twenty irate water organisms clambered to the edge of the water, snarling at the group. Harry was returning their earlier mimicking, as he knew they were safe on the land.

Jimmy, however, saw something alarmingly different to the others. Jimmy saw one of the organisms standing out from the crowd; he had a softer face than the others and had features he knew. This organism pushed past the group, walked out of the water, and approached Jimmy.

Jimmy knew this wasn't right and looked at his companions, who just carried on what they were doing as though they couldn't see the transparent creature boldly emerging from the water. Jimmy was already sitting down and put his arms behind his body, desperately trying to crawl away. He was doing all he could to escape, and the sheer fear on his face showed it. The rest of the group didn't even notice Jimmy's reaction.

"Calm down, Jimmy," said the creature, spitting water at him. "It's me, your father; I was killed when it wasn't my time in a way which wasn't written. I will not leave this realm until that time. I am *slowwwwwllyy* learning to maintain my *formmmm*, *bbeee* careful *iiiiit'sss noooottttt …*" The apparition melted into a puddle on the floor as Jimmy stretched his arm out to touch him one last time.

The soul of Jimmy's father was locked in the spirit realm and was learning how to maintain his form. Jimmy smiled to himself and knew his father was still here somewhere, but it made him deathly angry to know he was taken from Jimmy before his time and that his father could not move on. Talula, grabbing his arm, halted Jimmy's attention. Still panting at the fun they were having mimicking the organisms, she said, "Why are you looking so strange with your arm out? What are you doing?"

Solemnly, giving a glimpse of a smile, he said "Nothing, let's go."

Jimmy shouted to the others, "Come on, we need to get moving! We need to find where we are going."

Dusting himself off Jimmy looked at the map, which, during the excitement, he had unintentionally scrunched up. Unravelling it Jimmy saw, to his amazement, that it was blank; nothing at all, just an empty canvas.

The only thing that remotely matched was the tear down the middle. Jimmy found the other piece in his pocket, pulling it out. The ancient fabrics were identical in size, texture and colour. What he didn't understand was why the second piece was blank.

Scratching his head Jimmy looked closely and pushed both pieces together.

Instantly a line of fire zigzagged along the tear line and as the pieces merged, ink lines appeared in the same ink as the opposite page. The lines darted across the page and swirled as the invisible strokes drew buildings, rock formations and crossroads. The magical pen suddenly stopped and Jimmy could feel his face being dragged into the map.

Looking up, Harry was also being stretched into the map, as were Talula and Percy. Jimmy couldn't resist, the magic pulling him was too powerful and with a snap he was sucked in with the force of gravity forcing him into a severe, uncontrollable downward spiral.

Jimmy tried to look around the void but there was complete black emptiness apart from a few tiny silver stars, a silver half-moon and other distant unexplored planets blurring past his face. Jimmy was being forced at great speed into the unknown. The magical pull felt as though he was a piece of metal being summoned by a giant magnet.

Within a matter of seconds he felt the solid ground beneath his feet, but there was no sudden crash landing. It felt as though time had just stopped around him. He felt sick and dizzy from the wild roller coaster experience, but managed to compose himself. Quickly he gathered his bearings and saw that the others hadn't had such successful landings; they were lying on top of each other in a pile, with Percy leaning over the side to be sick. Jimmy helped them up, and then looked around at their new surroundings.

Chapter 20

The sky was the first thing that grabbed Jimmy's attention. The heavens were as red as blood crawling with evil, and angry purple clouds were screaming with the loud snaps of thunder rippling through the air. In the distance was the sound and smell of an imminent approaching storm.

Diverting their eyes from the remarkable view the group were standing in the shadow of a further deathly, yet awe inspiring view. In front of them in all its glory was a towering mountain face, which Jimmy instantly yet surprisingly knew. It was a view he had seen every day, but something was different; something was ghastly different.

The Blood Map had revealed to the group the true image of the normally pleasant, mundane mountain near to Jimmy's house. Jimmy couldn't believe the difference. It was as though he was looking at the mountain through the eyes of a demon.

Prominently in the middle of the creepy fearsome mountain now stood the deathly shape of a giant skull head. The empty black eyes of the skull stared back at the group, and perched on the bone sockets sat two pure black ravens, squawking to themselves. Two sharply pointed horns graced the top of the skull's head and with a fearsome scream the giant teeth and jaw opened slowly, revealing a dark yet vast cave entrance.

Jimmy could feel himself shaking but quickly whispered to his equally petrified companions, "I walked past here last year and it didn't look anything like this. There must have been a perception filter like the one next to the stables. The Blood Map must be the key to open it. This has to be Blackskull Mountain."

A groan rumbled from deep within the skull, quickly followed by a flash of fire which illuminated the cave and the path forward.

Whilst standing still, too scared to move in case the skull came alive and attacked them, a bolt of lightning crackled right above the skull, making the group jump backwards into a defensive stance and sending the crows soaring into the sky. Jimmy calmed himself down, once again checking his surroundings. Jimmy was the first to notice that as the group was facing the skull cave entrance they were also standing in between two huge stone bull statues forged in an aggressive forward facing stance. To Jimmy they looked like some sort of oversized decorative ornaments.

Harry moved first. Creeping towards the illuminated entrance he stood just before the darkness when he was startled as the two horns on top of the skull spun around quickly and revealed that they were in fact two stone gargoyles.

The gargoyles looked like the imps the group had conjured many times before, but with large dragon like wings folded up which gave the visual perspective from the rear of sharp horns. As Jimmy approached, to his and the group's surprise, the eyes of the stone creatures illuminated fiery red and their faces came alive. The gargoyle on the left was first to speak, in a squeaky high pitched voice.

"You there kids, haha, I am Monti, this is my stone brother Cornelius. We are the watchers of this cave tasked to make sure those stupid humans don't stumble into it!"

"Haha. *Yesss*," said the other gargoyle, Cornelius, "are you stupid humans? You look like it, haha!"

Cornelius turned, grinding its stone head to look at Monti.

"What do you think, Monti? They look like stupid humans to me: off with you, stupid humans, go on! Hahaha!"

Harry reacted in his normal aggressive tone.

"Listen, stones! We were brought here by the Blood Map and come in search of the Amulet of Trident!"

Both gargoyles chuckled on their perches, "Haha, *sooo* you search for the Trident do you? It must be that time already, how time flies, haha, Cornelius, do they look like the last lot? What do you think?"

"No, Monti, they look a lot stupider haha. Stupid looking children, you must prove your worth to enter the cave. We were placed here a great number of centuries ago by Lord Trident. We were tasked to provide this place with a filter. Stupid humans walk past here most days but they can only see a beautiful sky and a boring old mountain. For fun we do give them a rainbow now and again or a little rain haha, they never suspect a thing. But you four, you four were brought here like the others, you can see all. Perhaps you aren't like the stupid ones; perhaps you may try the test to enter!"

"And what is the test?" asked Talula impatiently.

"Haha, the test!" said Monti, "is to solve our riddle. If you fail you will be destroyed, hahaha, do you want the test?" Monti turned to Cornelius, "What do you think brother, shall we give them the test?"

"No," said Cornelius. "I think these are stupid humans just like the others, be gone! Haha!"

"No, no brother, they have the map, they must be allowed to try the riddle, try the riddle haha. Should they fail, then we have our fun!"

"Hmmm," grumbled Cornelius, "well, brother, if you insist."

With that the two strange, enchanted gargoyles spun a full circle and both their eyes changed to bright yellow.

"Children," said Monti, "your riddle to enter Blackskull Mountain –

"What goes around the house and in the house but never touches the house?"

The two gargoyles spun on the spot, continuously laughing, chanting to themselves, "They will never get it, they will never get it hahaha!"

The group looked at each other and repeated the riddle over and over. Harry and Percy gave a blank look, Talula and Jimmy looked endlessly into space. They continued to look for a few minutes without a real answer when Talula shouted,

"I've got it!" The gargoyles stopped spinning and gazed at Talula.

"The answer we need girl, the answer!"

Talula shouted, "The Moon!"

The gargoyles again proceeded to spin on the spot, laughing even louder,

"HAHAHAHA wrong, Corneluis they are stupid humans, hahaha!"

Monti stopped. "So stupid humans, the answer was wrong, the answer was the Sun. It rotates round the house, enters the house, but will never touch it. The Moon never enters the house as it's too dark, haha now you will be …"

There was a loud smash and Monti exploded into a pile of rubble, which dropped slowly bit by bit to the floor. It took the group a few seconds to register what had taken place when they turned and saw that Harry Hopkins had sent a beam of intense light straight at the gargoyle, causing it to explode in a blaze of fire. The group could see the anger in his eyes as he replied in an aggressive tone, "We are not 'stupid humans', this is taking too long; the cave door is open, we can just walk in!"

Cornelius tuned and saw his brother had been destroyed. "Noooo! My brother! What have you done?" His eyes illuminated red and he projected a thin laser beam past the group, straight into the eyes of the stone bull positioned to the right.

The stone covering the bull began to crack and crumble to the floor. In one swift motion the mighty beast tore his left leg from the stone slab, slamming it on the ground, quickly followed by his other three enormous thick, powerful legs. Snorting, the bull charged full speed at the group with its razor sharp horns pointing forward like daggers.

Reacting quickly the group dived out of the way as the enraged bull smashed straight into the second bull, completely obliterating it. The three youths looked at Harry: "What have you done, Harry? You didn't need to do that!" shouted Talula.

Moments later the bull was fiercely charging at the group once more.

Feeling responsible for his actions Harry stood his ground and sent a series of beams flying toward the bull;

all hit the stone beast in the face, causing a few fragments of stone dust to drift away. The impact momentarily blinded the bull causing it to veer off, missing Harry and hitting a large tree full on instead.

Shaking its head and yanking its horns free after being lodged in the trunk it turned to face the group and started to aggressively drag his right hoof backwards along the ground to show an imminent charge.

In a flash the bull set off again, narrowly missing the group after more blinding discharge from Harry.

This time the bull hit a large rock head on which caused the rock to split straight down the middle. The impact dazed the bull as it blew steam out of his nostrils in pure rage. The creature quickly determined that this was not the best form of attack as the youths were simply moving out of the way. The group looked on and watched as the creature stood still on the spot and they wondered what it was doing.

The stone creature started to make a cracking and creaking noise as though it was a machine moving for the first time. Rubble started crumbling to the floor and to the amazement of the group its front legs snapped in the opposite direction with a crunch that reverberated through the giant mountain. With one last thrust the beast snapped its legs upward, creating an elbow joint and as its legs bent forward, it forced itself up from the floor and was now standing on its two rear legs like a humongous human.

The bull, now standing upright, snorted at the group and began violently beating its chest whilst towering over them. The bull staggered to the stone structure where he had been originally set in place and smashed it with his right forearm. The structure split into four pieces and from within the rubble the creature pulled out a large wooden handled axe with a razor sharp blade covering the length of the weapon. The creature held the weapon in both arms high above his head and gave a roar, sending a shudder of fear through the children, as they knew this was going to be a long and dangerous battle.

Percy gave a nervous laugh at his companions and said, "I'm not sure I like these new lives of ours, it gets worse each time we fight someone ..."

Harry gave a nod, "Well, let's get messy then."

Harry sent an intense beam of blazing light cascading toward the chest of the creature, causing it to stagger backwards as small fragments of its body crumbled to the floor. The bull regained its footing and began rotating the giant axe above his head like a helicopter propeller and bounded forward.

Jimmy also sent a series of lightning bolts at the beast, but they had less of an effect than Harry's.

Talula started to chant the Mirosharr language; two Toad warriors emerged from the ground and charged forward, swords and shields raised. The others also gave the same chant and in total eight toads ran at the stone beast. The first toad to arrive was chopped down in full charge. The second managed to strike the beast with its sword which simply shattered on impact. The beast made very light work of the others.

Harry shouted at Percy to hold him off whilst he took a step back from the group and rummaged through his pockets. In reply, Percy morphed into the giant dragon, flew in the air around the stone bull and sent a projectile of fire, encasing the beast completely. The stone covering the creature didn't crack or blister; it was having no effect at all. The dragon continued to swoop closer and closer until a strike from the bull clipped Percy's wing, causing him to lose his flight and send him crashing to the ground.

By this time Harry had found what he wanted; the Nightstalker scroll.

"*Nierro, Nierro,*" he commanded at the top of his voice, whilst shaking through fear and adrenaline, giving the chant all of his focus.

A giant lizard creature suddenly grew from the ground next to Jimmy. The giant green lizard with its long armour covered tail was the same height as the bull and instantly leaped from its standing position into the stone warrior and locked arms in a struggle of immense power. It was the battle of an unstoppable force versus an immovable object.

The two creatures battled, with the group also assisting with wave after wave of attack. After a few moments the creatures demonstrated equal strength and simply pushed each other away.

In the same motion as being pushed apart from the bull the lizard turned in mid flow and whipped his tail forcefully into the chest of the bull with such an impact that the bull fell straight to the floor in a heap.

Seizing its chance to end the battle the lizard approached the vulnerable bull and angled its body for another whipping action at the stone creature's head. The reptile was in full swing but was stopped mid flow and was dragged screaming back into the earth.

The group stared at Harry, but he shook his head and said, "It's gone, I-I couldn't hold it any longer, the spell was too powerful!"

Panicking, the group started to fire at the bull again, but it slowly returned to its feet, picked up the axe and once again approached the group wildly swinging its destructive weapon.

Talula had been assisting her friends as much as she could but was looking around trying to find a different way to defeat the creature. The others were continuing to fire wave after wave of attack because although it was having no real effect, small amounts of stone were falling off and the reasoning was that if they attacked for long enough there wouldn't be any stone left.

Then, Talula had a thought. *Why wasn't the second bull attacking? It had been smashed to pieces by the first bull but why hadn't it come alive? Was it because the first gargoyle had been destroyed and therefore its life force was ended?*

Talula looked beyond the approaching bull and saw the other gargoyle's eyes flickering between yellow and red. She had an idea and filled with confidence ran directly at the charging bull. The beast raised its axe over its right shoulder, ready to swing, but as Talula approached she dived forward, morphing mid-flight into a bat. Talula flew over the head of the beast, reverting back and landing whilst still running on the other side. Talula ran as fast as she could and formed a small fireball in her hands; as she approached the entrance to the cave, she fired straight at the cowering gargoyle.

Instantly it exploded in a rain of fire and ash and Talula skidded to a halt. She turned in time to see Jimmy launch a lightning bolt straight at the chest of the creature. The beast staggered backwards a step, and then dropped to its knees. Percy had regained his strength after the giant stone bull had injured him. Just after the bull's knees touched the floor simultaneously Percy morphed into the dragon once again and ferociously swung with his razor clawed right arm, taking the head of the stone creature clean off.

The stone head rolled like a boulder landing square at the feet of Talula. The eyes were still blinking open and shut. Talula could see the detail that had gone into the sculpture, including the nose ring; but it had chosen to attack them. The group looked at the beast's body and it imploded with raging red fire from within, sending red-hot shards across the air like mini meteors.

Talula re-joined the group. They were all exhausted; they were covered in black dust and grime, had torn clothing and were simply battered and bruised. Jimmy spoke first.

"This much trouble and we haven't entered the cave yet. Harry, in future think or consult us before you go off and do things. You almost got us killed!"

"Hey, we all failed the stupid riddle, we didn't know what power that gargoyle had; it could have destroyed us or sent us to a black hole or anything, I saved us!" said Harry.

"Calm down, both of you," said Talula, "we have survived and got this far by working together; we all bring something to this team and it is working, don't let us fight and make matters worse.

"We need to rest a while, I don't think we are in a fit state to go rushing into the cave, we have no idea who or what is in there."

"I agree," said Percy, still applying pressure to the cut he had received on his right forearm from the beast's strike.

"We have worked well here in getting this far, don't spoil things, let's all calm down and have five minutes out," Talula concluded.

Jimmy approached Percy and walked him off to the area where the second bull had been standing. He sat Percy down and tore a strip of cloth from his trouser leg and wrapped it around the cut whilst applying pressure.

"Percy, this journey has taken its toll on us. We have been lucky so many times, I'm worried that next time we won't be that lucky and something bad will happen ..."

"Jimmy, you worry too much, Lyreco has told us that it has been foretold we will replenish the earth. I trust him and the rest of you with my life. Whatever awaits us in that cave we will overcome it; we are growing stronger by the day."

Talula approached the two of them and beckoned Jimmy toward her. Jimmy stood, checking on Percy's arm again.

"It's okay Jimmy, I'll be fine, I'll just rest here."

Jimmy walked to Talula and he saw in the distance that Harry was starting to make a fire with the branches that had fallen when the bull hit the tree, and surrounded it with the rocks from the smashed stone plates.

"Jimmy, I am sorry I broke up your argument, but it was getting heated and I was afraid you may start to fight each other. Harry is very hot headed and will often dive straight in. You were right to speak to him about it, but he clearly doesn't react well to criticism."

"Don't worry, Talula, I can handle myself and Harry if needed. You did well to think about other ways to kill that beast. I don't think any of us would have even considered smashing the gargoyle."

Talula smiled. "It was nothing, I just wondered why the second bull didn't attack, and then I took a gamble. I would have looked really stupid if it hadn't paid off."

Jimmy looked at the floor.

"Talula, I am worried about what lies ahead in that cave. There could be anything in there, any dangers; I don't want any of us to get hurt, especially you ..."

"Come on Jimmy, I'll be fine, we work well together as a group and we have beaten some really serious foes. Nothing will stop us. We will retrieve the Amulet of Trident, gain more and more power and achieve our destiny. Then we can defeat the Elders and start this world again, right this time, in our image, not that of the Elders."

"Talula, you can't be serious, is that your plan? That's madness!"

"It's not; you heard what Lady Aurabella said. She did what they asked and then they cast the previous four youths out like they were nothing, to live a life of sorrow! I will do their bidding, I will become more powerful than anyone. I will destroy this world, destroy the Elders and we will rule this place together!"

Taken back by this revelation, Jimmy didn't respond. He had never seen or heard Talula like this. Jimmy didn't want to destroy this world. He didn't want all of this raw power, but in the pit of his stomach there was an insatiable thirst for revenge, and he needed to continue until the Gatekeeper was destroyed.

Chapter 21

The group rested for a number of hours before they decided that the time was right to see what fate Blackskull Mountain held for them.

Leaving the fire roaring in case they needed to escape in a hurry and could use its light as a guide, the group, led by Harry, tentatively walked into the mouth entrance of the cave.

Jimmy was the last to walk in and as he did he looked up and saw some words carved in red blood on the rock above the entrance. The wording was '*Dayar Menuez Laylantoss*'.

As he looked at the words they started to shake and the letters began to move about and change until the sign read, *Only the virtuous will prosper*.

Jimmy grabbed Talula by the arm and gently pulled her back,

"What does that say?"

Talula stared for a few seconds at the letters and said,

"Just some old letters, nothing really. Come on!"

Jimmy was dragged into the cave but kept thinking to himself, *why can I see those words but the others can't? What does 'only the virtuous will prosper' mean?*

Just before Jimmy stepped out of view he had the sudden urge to glance over his shoulder. There in the short distance was the owl again, the owl that had been following him since the start. The owl flew upward from the tree flying high above the mountain and out of his sight. Jimmy's sleeve was tugged and he was dragged into the cave.

The group walked down the solid granite marble steps. The air was thin and stale, with an undisputable smell of decay and destruction. It was pitch black apart from a few torches lit by a slight flickering flame and a bright fire leading the way. Each step had large cracks continuously running across them, worn through the ages. There were cobwebs all over the walls, banisters and on a few occasions spanning directly across the walkway. The group walked face first into a few of them and received a mouth full of sticky webbing and ancient dead flies. No one had visited this cave in centuries.

The cave was icy cold, with a chilling air whistling in from the mouth of the skull. Every time the group took a breath the freezing air burnt their lungs and as the condensation puffed out of their mouths it quickly evaporated through the tiny cracks in the wall.

"What is this place?" said Percy, "I don't like this, it's like there is something watching and following us, the place just feels wrong ..."

"Don't be silly; come on, keep going. We have done the hard bit getting this far," said Harry, leading the others.

Talula turned back to Jimmy. "Why do you keep looking behind you? What is it?"

"Nothing, it's okay, I'm, um, just checking to make sure nothing is coming in behind us, that's all."

The group descended the stairs, going deeper and deeper into the darkness until they finally reached the bottom.

As the group stepped from the last stone slab they heard it. A terrifying voice echoed all around and even through them. The voice was loud, deep, and raspy; enough to send a chill down the spine of the group and raise the hairs on their arms.

"Children, you have arrived! You have done well to find Blackskull Mountain. Your search for the Amulet of Trident is nearly at its end, but be warned, this will be your darkest journey. Some of you may not survive.

"You must pass a series of deathly challenges, and then only the worthy will succeed and enter Trident's throne room and collect the Amulet."

On his final word a gust of air swept through the room and momentarily blew out the flickering lights, before they immediately relit themselves.

The group looked at each other.

"Who or what was that? There isn't supposed to be anyone else down here, who is talking?"

Percy was talking very quickly and at the time his eyes were darting around the room, trying not to show his fear.

When the lights flickered back on the group were standing in the middle of a grand, open cubed stronghold with damp and cold stone walls surrounding them. At the far end of the room the wall had been destroyed or had crumbled though time. Beyond the hole was black, lifeless emptiness; in front of which was a pile of large cubed stones and rubble. This was the only way forward.

With a poof of smoke Jimmy illuminated his arm and his pure green flame ignited the room. Slowly he moved around in a circle, checking each corner, but there were no other doors and nothing of any real significance.

Once Jimmy had walked the circumference he reluctantly walked to the hole, climbing over the rubble. Thrusting his illuminated hand into the vast darkness, there was nothing on the other side apart from a ledge just large enough for one person to stand. Squeezing himself through the tight gap his elbow glanced a loose stone causing it to fall to the ground, showering the air with dust. The sound echoed through the vast empty canyon, startling Jimmy as he nearly lost his balance and fell into the abyss. At the last second he reached out with his hand and grabbed the top of a round metal sign dug into the ledge.

"The wall isn't safe. Be careful when you crawl through."

Taking a deep breath to compose himself he looked at the curious sign, which he was sure hadn't been there when he had stepped onto the ledge.

Wiping off the thick layer of dust Jimmy saw that the sign read,

Unearthly Rail Company Limited.
Next train in approximately 2 minutes.
Please stand a safe distance from the track.

Looking puzzled Jimmy thought; *track, what track?*

Jimmy shone his light out into the emptiness and as he did sparkling silver train tracks darted from the edge of the ledge and jetted out as far as Jimmy could see. The tracks were simply floating in mid-air.

Staring into the distance Jimmy felt the ledge vibrating and small grains of rubble started dancing across the dusty floor. The vibration became stronger and stronger and in the distance he could hear the *choo choo* sound of a train as a thick cloud of steam blocked his view. Jimmy didn't have time to turn and speak to his companions. The cloud tore open and from within raced a huge black locomotive, heading at full speed toward the ledge.

The giant steel jaws of the train's grille were getting closer and closer, but it didn't slow down and Jimmy had to shield his eyes due to the blinding lights burning his retinas.

Raising his hand and trying to look at the raging machine, panic flooded his body. He had nowhere to go, nowhere to hide; the ledge was barely enough to stand on. Jimmy watched in horror and moved his footing, ready to dive back into the previous room, but it was too late. The train was coming too fast for Jimmy to react.

Closing his eyes in sheer desperation, the train drove straight off the edge of the tracks, passed through Jimmy like a ghost and bumped into the damaged wall head on. Still squeezing his eyes shut with all his might Jimmy opened one of them to see what had happened.

Instead of a disastrous train collision, which would have destroyed the whole structure, the train merely bounced off of the wall. Like a ghost the front end of the train simply coiled backwards through the other static carriages and when it reached the back end, snapped 180 degrees instantly facing the opposite way. In one swift bouncing motion the train had gone from almost crashing, to completely turning itself around and was now ready to go again facing the other direction.

Jimmy looked on in sheer disbelief. Trying to work out what had just happened he looked at the front of the train when a small, clean, white skull head stuck out of the front driver's compartment and shouted, "All aboard! Next stop Fatality Canyon, all aboard!"

WOOP WOO! echoed around the building as the unnatural driver pulled the horn.

Jimmy knew the others wouldn't have seen the grand entrance, but knew they would have heard it.

Talula pushed her head out. "Jimmy, what was that?"

Shouting back, Jimmy allowed his heart rate to get back to normal. "It's some sort of train, come on, get in, one at a time though, and be careful."

Jimmy walked to the edge of the ledge where the last shining red carriage had stopped and warily put his hand out, grabbing onto the train; he wasn't sure what to expect. Jimmy's hand merged through wet, sticky electro plasma and when he put his hand on the carriage itself, he found it was plain old wood.

Holding on tight he pulled his body through the plasma and through the wooden train carriage entrance and sat down. He expected it to be wet and covered in the slime, but to his surprise it was bone dry. The others slowly followed through the gap and one by one took their seat on the train. Percy was the last through and the instant his back touched the rear of his seat, he gasped in surprise.

Woooshhhh! The train darted off at immense speed.

The force and speed caused the group's heads to be pinned to the back of their seats as they soared at immense speed upwards, then dramatically downward, at one stage spinning in a spiral that sent the rattling carriage upside down.

The train felt like a wild roller coaster ride and some of the group started to feel sick at the speed and uncontrolled motion. They tried to turn their heads to see what was going on around them but they were pinned in place and the scenery was a blur.

The unnatural journey continued in this fashion for a further five minutes when suddenly the carriage door swung open and in staggered the skull headed driver who had told Jimmy to board the train.

The skull was attached to a long spindly skeleton wearing a blue cap and blue overalls which both portrayed the logo *Unearthly Rail* and had *day conductor* written in yellow cotton underneath.

"Tickets please, all tickets please!" was the continuous chant he hollered as he walked up the aisle. The ghastly conductor would periodically stop at the seats before him, take an imaginary ticket and stamp it.

The train conductor finally approached the group of youths and again shouted, "Tickets please, all tickets please!"

Percy snapped a quick reply, "We, we don't have a ticket? We didn't see anywhere to buy one …"

"NO TICKET! NO TICKET! STOP THE TRAIN!"

The conductor reached out his long, thin fingers above his head and pulled down hard on the emergency stop wire. The train instantly fell into a dramatic nosedive along the track and was heading at full speed towards an area of ground that was fast approaching and getting bigger and bigger.

The train made no movement towards slowing down and continued to the ground at warp speed. The group, grabbing each other and scared out of their wits, braced for an immediate impact and thrust their hands over their eyes.

Peering through the gaps in their fingers they were surprised to see the front of the train go through the ground like a ghost through a wall. The next carriage darted, then the beginning of their carriage, then up to their feet and instantly they could feel the ground beneath them and the remainder of the train flowing over the top of them.

The train had gone through the ground, come out at the other side and then veered back upwards, but the group had been placed gently on the ground. The group looked at the train flowing away from them at full speed and saw the conductor on the back of the train carriage waving his fist at them shouting, "NO TICKET! NO TRIP!"

Seconds later the train was out of sight.

"What was that all about?" said Percy. "This place is madness, free roaming trains from which you get kicked off for not having a ticket which you can't buy, talking caves, evil gargoyles?"

"Yeah, I didn't like that; I thought we were goners … again. So where do we go from here?" Talula frowned.

As an almost instant response to the last question a wooden sign pushed its way out of the ground with an arrow pointing forward which read,

Fatality Canyon.

With no further suggestions the group walked on, following the mysterious sign.

Chapter 22

The group trekked along the brown dusty path for about an hour until they eventually saw a grand, stone entrance towering in the distance. As the group approached the opening, it was clear it was just a stone frame supporting a huge marble beam to create the doorway.

To the surprise of the group no structure or support could be seen on either side or behind. It was just a stone doorframe in the middle of a canyon.

Percy thrust his hand into the doorway and peered around the frame and found that his hand couldn't be seen on the other side. Looking beyond the doorframe as far as he could into the distance, Percy saw that there was nothing else. The path they were following stretched onward into the unknown.

"This must be some sort of mystical portal. There is nothing else anywhere around it, but it leads somewhere. My hand disappeared. Come on, I'm going in. I want to see where it leads!"

Trepidation rose within Talula. She grabbed Jimmy's arm. "I don't like this. This … this place, it doesn't feel right …"

Jimmy took hold of her hand. "Come on, Talula, we've got this far. There is nowhere else to go. We can't go back, this is the only door. This must be the right way. Come on, you go through ahead of me and I'll make sure nothing appears behind us?"

Each member stepped through the doorway and disappeared. Jimmy followed last and as he did he heard the faint sound of scraping above his head. Glancing up at the black, reflective marble beam he once again saw unusual letters scratched into the surface in the same language as before. The stone beam vibrated and the letters changed into something he could read,

Only the pure of heart can progress.

But what does it mean? I need to figure it out and quick. I think Talula was right. This place is creepy. It feels like something is watching us. But where can it hide? Pull yourself together, Jimmy! Thoughts raced through Jimmy's mind and, checking over his shoulder one last time, he stepped through the doorway behind his companions.

With a blaze of light, a wave of steamed air flooded past his face as he stepped into the back of Harry, who was frozen in place by fright and trembling through fear. The path they had been following was gone and replaced by a thin tightrope of crumbling stone suspended over a vast, endless canyon. The path was barely wide enough for one person to carefully shuffle across.

To make matters worse the middle section of the stone path had completely eroded away over time. The gap was far too wide and unstable to jump, but it was the only way forward. As the group delicately looked over their shoulders, holding each other for balance, they looked at the door they had just walked through. The dread of realisation flooded over them when in front of their gazing view the black rectangular vortex faded away, revealing an even longer damaged path heading in the other direction. The vibrations from the collapsing vortex shook the path behind them as the fragile ground crumbled and disintegrated into the darkness.

"Looks like forward it is, then …" said Percy with a slight tremble in his voice.

Jimmy felt his hand being squeezed really tightly and as he looked at Talula, she realised what she was doing and snatched it away, refusing to show fear in front of the others.

Percy, at the front of the group, slowly tottered to the edge and looked down into the endless darkness. Bending down to pick up a stone lying on the floor he dropped it into the enormous hole. The group waited and listened but the rock never hit the bottom.

Percy was startled and quickly stepped away from the canyon as the eerie voice resonated around the cavern.

"Children, you have reached the first challenge. Fatality Canyon. You must cross the damaged canyon on your own. Only then will you be granted access to the next challenge."

As the group looked at each other, Jimmy was first to speak, "How are we going to get across that? There's no bridge, rope, nothing?"

"There seems to be only one way …" said Talula, "We have to change to our inner creatures and fly across. Harry, you are going to have to wait here."

"No way, I'm more valuable than any of you to this journey. You need me, what if we get attacked again, you need my power!" argued Harry.

Talula was quick to reply, "How are you going to get across then? You're a snake, you can't fly!"

"I may be a snake, but that means I'm light. Percy is the biggest; he can carry me with no effort at all!"

"I don't like this, the instructions were specific …" nervously replied Talula.

"You need me; we are doing it, so let's go!"

The group members simultaneously transformed into their inner creatures.

Jimmy morphed into the fiery green phoenix, Talula into the black bat, Percy the yellow and blue dragon and Harry the black viper. The three winged creatures took flight and Percy swooped down, collecting the coiled viper in its talons.

The creatures flew high above the gorge, making their way across the canyon. After travelling over the half-way point Jimmy's confidence grew and he started to believe it was going to work. He shouted to his companions, "We are doing so well. Nothing is attacking us; it looks like we will be fine …"

Flying a little further, Talula and Jimmy approached the far side of the canyon. Soaring at speed they turned to each other just as they passed through another wobbling, plasma barrier, which they hadn't noticed until they were pushed through to the other side.

They both heard the soft, sludgy pop as the barrier closed behind them. A fiery sensation burnt them both from head to toe and their mystical inner creatures slowly faded away. Their momentum was the only thing pushing them through the air. In a heartbeat, Jimmy felt the grip of an invisible hand and he was catapulted with sheer force, hurtling toward the ledge. He landed, skidding to a halt and using his elbow as a brake. Turning to look over his shoulder he saw Talula skidding past him, leaving a trail of cavern dust covering Jimmy as it swept over him.

They both rolled over and looked back. They knew something was wrong.

Something was disastrously wrong. Percy watched in terror as his two companions flew through the field and were changed back to their human form only to be launched forward.

It was too late for Percy to stop. Instantly, he felt his giant wings becoming tired and he was dragged slightly downward, losing immediate altitude. Percy flapped faster as hard as he could, but he was being pulled into the rift.

Frantically he looked down into the unknown, but there was nothing, just the snake clenched between his talons.

Percy struggled on, but was dragged down again. It felt as if a ton of weight had been added to the snake, then another. Percy was buckling under the pressure, but knew he couldn't fail; he had to succeed for his companions, for the mission.

Through sheer determination he dragged himself forward, reaching the plasma shield.

Little did Percy know this was the worst thing he could have done, but the only option he had. The instant he touched the distorted field his inner creature was sucked out of him and he changed back to his human form. He was then catapulted, with the same velocity as the others had been, sent spiralling through the air and landing in front of Jimmy and Talula.

The story was not the same for Harry. Hitting the barrier as a viper, he was flung forward into his human form but just beyond the plasma field, the air turned into a solid, invisible brick wall. Crashing into the wall with a mighty thump, time stood still until he slid down at a great speed.

As a last ditch attempt Harry clambered with his fingers and managed to grab onto the edge of the canyon. Instinctively, Jimmy quickly got up and ran over skidding on his hands and knees and managed to reach out and grab his companion's right wrist.

In the background they could hear Talula screaming, "Harry!"

Jimmy had a strong grip and tried to pull Harry upward, but he couldn't move him. Harry was dazed from the impact and was trying his best to pull himself up, but something was terribly wrong.

Harry hollered in pain and, looking down, saw that his feet, the bottom of his legs, and then the top of his legs were turning to stone. Jimmy held on for dear life but within seconds the stone encased Harry, reaching his elbow. Through sheer weight Jimmy couldn't sustain his grip any longer. It was a moment that Jimmy would never forget. Harry's face when he had to release his hold or be dragged into the void with him.

There was nothing else Jimmy could do. He let go of Harry's hand and as he started to fall he saw the stone crawl over him until there were no human features left. Percy regained his composure and ran over to assist Jimmy, but he was only in time to see Harry fall silently out of sight. A lonely figure submerged in stone, free falling into the vast emptiness.

Jimmy pulled away from the edge and sat up, holding his hands over his open mouth; he couldn't believe it. What had he done? He had let his companion, no, his friend fall and he was never going to see him again. A wave of dread fell over him; *what does this mean? Have we failed our journey?*

Talula ran over and grabbed Jimmy, who was now sitting on the floor, and gave him a big hug. She had tears in her eyes and said the words that Jimmy needed to hear: "It wasn't your fault, you did everything you could. You had to let go or you would have been dragged into the void as well. I couldn't bear to lose you both!"

Jimmy held Talula close to him for as long as possible, he had never really experienced affection; someone caring about his feelings, well, it felt warm and pleasant.

"Come on you two, we have to carry on. We were told to cross the canyon alone. Harry took the risk by crossing it with me and now he is gone. We have to succeed ..."

Percy bent down and pulled them both to their feet. They sniffed, wiping their eyes and noses and, through sheer determination, carried on with their journey.

Chapter 23

The remaining three carried on their passage in silence. It felt surreal to them, one minute they were all together on their journey, the next, Harry was gone. They were all very young and had never really experienced death apart from Jimmy. They had thought they were indestructible, nothing had fazed them or could ever hurt them, but they had just been given a sharp pinch of reality.

The group walked along the black corridors, not knowing what dangers or mystical creatures lay in front of them. The cavern was never-ending and they seemed to be trudging along endless passages.

After a short while the group walked into a large room completely engulfed with darkness. Jimmy walked into the room onto a cold stone floor and he felt the slab beneath him lower into the ground slowly, as though he had pressed an invisible button. The anxiety quickly surged through his body and he jumped into a defensive position, ready for any imminent attack.

Before he had time to shout to his companions, two continuous streams of red-hot flame illuminated between the two corners behind them, blocking the door by which they had just entered. The room was large, open, covered with stone slabs all around, but there was no other door.

At the opposite side of the room stood three giant stone statues. The statues wore Saxon helmets, chiselled armour and held a giant shield in their left hands. In their right hands, firmly gripped, was a colossal sword held facing downward with the tip lodged into the supporting slab of stone.

"How do we get out of here?" said Talula as she walked to the statues, touching one of them. Rubbing her fingers along the solid stone warrior, nothing happened.

"Perhaps we have to smash them to get past?" said Percy as he kicked another of the giant guards.

Jimmy carried on talking to his companions and leant on the arm of the final guard to rest for a moment.

"I don't know, are we *mii—arhh*!"

The room violently rumbled as Jimmy swiftly pulled his arm away from his resting post. The touch had sent a chain reaction shaking through the guard. The handprint he had left illuminated fiery red and streams of thin red cracks darted throughout the stone bodies of the guards.

Within seconds the crack lines reached the eyes of all three stones guards. Their eyes ignited in a sea of red and with the scraping of stone on stone, each warrior turned its head to look at the group.

The ground rumbled again with particles of dust and stone fragments falling from the ceiling. One by one the giant stone warriors were sucked through a doorway behind them, which their gigantic frames had covered. The guards flew into the air before flying backwards a short distance away, landing at the far side of three ancient, long, thin rickety wooden rope bridges.

The group passed cautiously through the newly revealed entrance. The three long bridges led across another black abyss, leading to a path on the far side.

The question racing through their minds now, was how they would get past the guards.

As they thought about it the deathly voice echoed through the cave.

"You have done well to get this far, this is the next challenge. You each have a bridge highlighted by a dragon, bat or phoenix. You must step onto the bridge to start. The guard is attuned to your life force and will mirror your every movement. When you run forward onto the bridge, the guard will follow you. You must find a way of getting past them ... Alive! HAHAHA!" and with that, there was silence.

The group looked at each other but, after what happened to Harry, didn't dare to break the rules as they had in the last challenge. They had seen the deathly consequences. From the position of the group Percy could see his bridge with the dragon emblem on top of a wooden stake in the ground. Percy sheepishly looked at the group, and then walked to the beginning of the old rope bridge. Talula and Jimmy walked forward, staying close together until Talula noticed that she had the middle bridge. Jimmy walked to the third bridge, approached the wooden post and blew off the dust. True to his word, this post contained the image of a phoenix.

The group held off stepping on their bridges through fear of what may happen. Jimmy took a deep breath and crossed over the threshold. At the far end of the bridge, the stone guard's eyes pulsated and smoke billowed from his nose. The stone warrior mirrored Jimmy and hovered forward. Jimmy stepped to the right and the guard hovered to his left.

Percy had other ideas. He didn't cross the line but sent a stream of red-hot fire along the bridge into the stone guardian's head. He held his power for a few moments but nothing happened, no movement, no damage, not even smoke. Trying again he stepped forward and the guard sprang into life, as smoke hissed from his creaking joints.

Talula had also stepped forward but didn't dare move again until they all knew what to do.

Jimmy had an idea. Holding onto the frail rope and watching his footing on the rotten wooden slats, he climbed over the other side of the bridge. The guard wasn't fooled. In reply it propelled high above the bridge and simply moved across, hovering above the void facing Jimmy. Jimmy instantly knew this was a bad idea and quickly clambered back over before he fell. Whilst looking down he noticed that there was pure emptiness below them and he didn't want to be the one to fall.

Talula took another step forward and fired a fireball. This staggered the guard and sent some rubble crumbling to the floor, but when she stepped backwards the guard took another step forward. Talula looked at Jimmy, and then at Percy.

Talula turned once more to Jimmy, giving a solemn look and smile as though this was going to be the end, and charged, screaming a war cry. Percy did the exact same thing as they both sent a stream of fire and aggression into the inanimate, colossal guardians.

As they approached, the stone creatures raised their shields to deflect the blasts. The warrior in the middle swung the sword downward with sheer velocity at Talula, narrowly missing and smashing a hole in the wooden slate.

Percy wasn't faring any better. He stood in front of the guard firing a blast of fire, trying anything he could to melt the stone. He was trying everything but the guard didn't budge.

Jimmy couldn't move. He didn't walk forward or back and just watched to see how his friends fared. He so wanted to help but there was nothing he could do. They each had to fight their own guard ... or did they?

The stone guards were thrusting their destructive swords, each swipe getting closer and quicker. The two youths' magical powers were having no effect. In pure desperation, Percy morphed into the dragon to give himself a height and power advantage.

The ropes screamed, tensing under the immense weight of the transformed beast. The mighty dragon struck the guard with a powerful claw, then another and another, but to no avail. The guard merely parried them with its shield. Not thinking of the consequences, Percy focused and let loose with a wave of smouldering fire intending to incinerate the stone opponent.

The fierce blast deflected off the guard's shield and set the fragile rope alight. In a flash the whole bridge was burning.

"Noooooo! Percy!" screamed Jimmy looking on, powerless to help.

A *pinging* noise reverberated through the canyon as the ropes snapped at either end of the fire ridden wooden bridge. Frozen in slow motion, the dragon and the stone guardian plummeted silently into the void.

Desperation and anger channelled through Jimmy, but he knew attacking the guard head on wasn't the answer. Talula was fighting valiantly and she didn't even notice what had happened to Percy. She was in a crouching position using all she had in her arsenal to hold off a downward sword thrust heading straight for her. Jimmy thought quickly and had a risky idea that would either save them both, or send them to their doom.

Selflessly Jimmy turned and as quick as he could ran back along the bridge the way he had come. He ran along the bridge, past the post, and headed toward Talula's bridge. He glanced as he ran and saw the guard was following him, but was hovering across the void flying parallel.

This was what Jimmy was banking on. Talula was getting weaker and weaker and the blade was getting closer. Before Jimmy approached the middle bridge he flung two bolts of lightning from his left and right hand in the direction of his guard.

Both narrowly missed and fizzled out in the distance behind the stone guard. Jimmy ran onto the bridge and in a mirrored response Jimmy's guard landed on the far side, trudging forward.

Talula's guard was giving all its attention to her and didn't notice Jimmy running towards it. The adrenalin was surging throughout Jimmy and his aggression was bubbling. He had already lost two friends; he wasn't about to lose a third.

Running along the wooden bridge at full speed he instantly let loose with one, two, and then three bolts of adrenalin-charged lightning. The unsuspecting guard looked up as the first bolt hit him square between the eyes, causing his head to rock back as his red jewel eyes shattered into a thousand pieces. The second caused even more devastation, taking the stone guard's head clean off and sending it rolling backwards to the now fast approaching second guard.

By the time the third bolt came, the now headless guard had raised his sword and shield to block it. The powerful distraction technique displayed by Jimmy had achieved its goal. The first guard was completely distracted and was no longer aggressively attacking Talula and the second was stuck behind the first.

Jimmy ran to Talula, grabbed the back of her robe, and helped her to her feet. He pushed her in front of him as they quickly made their way towards the beginning of the bridge where they had started.

Jimmy glanced back over his shoulder and the two stone guards were making their way quickly towards them.

Jimmy hollered to Talula, "When I shout jump! Jump, and hang on with every bit of strength you have."

Talula heard what he said and kept running as fast as she could. Jimmy gently jogged after her; when he was ready he turned and as time slowed once more he threw a bolt of lightning from his right arm towards the right shoulder of the approaching second guard.

The height of the bolt missed the first guard and went shooting straight over where his head would have been. The second guard reacted to the bolt and moved to its left. The bolt missed both warriors, spinning into the distance.

Jimmy screamed at the top of his voice, "Jump!!!"

Talula dived forward, landing face first into the wooden bridge, holding on for dear life. Jimmy jumped through the air and he thought to himself; *I bet they thought all the bolts I threw missed.*

He smiled to himself as he flew through the air.

SNAP!

Both ropes at the far side of the bridge behind the guards had snapped and the bridge was now in a free fall hurtling the bridge, Jimmy and Talula like a pendulum, heading face first into the ledge.

When Jimmy jumped he hadn't managed to land or hold onto the wooden slats, but momentum was still dragging him forward. At the last second he managed to claw onto Talula's right leg, and then gripped hold with his left hand.

Below he saw the bridge shoot from underneath him and the two guards falling helplessly to their demise. The pair were still in a pendulum swing, hurtling at great speed towards the jagged rock face. They both braced for impact and as they collided, Talula caught her face on the wall and Jimmy's shoulder hit the sharp rock. The bridge came to a stop and Talula was clinging on to a wooden slat with Jimmy dangling from her legs.

Jimmy tried his best not to look down into the dark void, but every time he did, a tremble of fear shot through his muscles and joints. In one last brave act he tried to use his left foot to hook a slat to support his weight. After a few attempts he pressed his foot onto a slat and brought down his right foot for support. Slowly he released one hand from Taluala's clothing and grabbed a loose slat behind her feet.

"Talula, try and pull yourself up the bridge, don't look down!"

Talula lifted her left arm up onto the slat above but could feel her whole body tremble. Slowly she pulled herself up the vertical bridge one slat at a time, with Jimmy clambering close behind.

After scaling ten of the slats with relative ease the confidence started to rise in Talula and she started to move a little quicker. She could see the top of the ledge and was five slats away. Reaching out with her left hand she grabbed the next slat, took a firm grip—and then disaster struck.

The wooden slat was rotten, and crumbled in her left hand. Her right hand had already moved forward to grab the next rung and in a split second she had lost all her grip and fell backward.

The ever-vigilant Jimmy saw her fall and flung his left arm out, more instinctively than anything else.

Luckily he grabbed hold of Talula's arm as she fell and, using the momentum, he pulled her into him; she safely clung on, breathing hard.

After that scare they were both more cautious as they began again to slowly claw their way back up the bridge together, collapsing in exhaustion when they finally reached the top.

Lying on her back, Talula was panting heavily when realisation hit her again. She turned, looking at Jimmy and although in her heart she already knew the answer, she asked just to make sure.

"Jimmy, where is Percy?" Jimmy solemnly looked at her.

A lump grew in the back of his throat.

In the excitement he had put the vision to the back of his mind, but he knew the answer.

"Talula, he is gone, there was nothing I could do. He fought the guard valiantly but the bridge burnt and he fell into the void. With his death I figured out a way to beat them, he didn't die in vain. When his guard fell I worked out that they could hover at a certain altitude, and only when they were expecting to hover.

"If they fell below that altitude or fell whilst they were preoccupied they wouldn't be able to propel back up. Without his valiance we would have died as well …"

Talula turned away to sob into her hands.

They had lost so much on this quest, and what had they gained? Nothing! Jimmy leant over to console her, but after only a few minutes he stood up and said, "Come on; I know this is hard, but we have come too far to give in now!"

Chapter 24

The lone pair carried on through the dreary cavern and were speaking less and less after the tragic events. The loss of their two companions hit Talula very hard. All she could do was think about Harry and Percy and how they had been lost in this wretched place. Looking at Jimmy her heart sank. *What if I lose him? I don't think I could cope with that or being on my own, I hate this place. I want to go home. I hate home but anything has to be better than dying alone in this dark, damp cave.*

As the two continued, Jimmy noticed they were now starting to walk upwards, where previously they had been going further and further down into the cave. They were walking up a stone ramp, and the further they climbed the thinner the ramp became, until they were walking single file and only had enough room for their two feet.

Eventually they reached a grand entrance door.

Jimmy looked above the door and once again there were words in a different language. The words rumbled and changed,

'Be True To Yourself'.

He had no idea what that meant but kept it in the back of his mind as they once again walked into the dark unknown.

Walking into the large room, the thud of their boots sent echoes resonating around the area. The room was illuminated with green fires floating high in the air without any form of support or fixture. The path in front of them was very thin and still only allowed room for them to walk in single file; but there was an insurmountable drop into the darkness below them.

Jimmy took the lead.

As the pair reached the half-way point of the path they saw that it led to a large saucer shaped stone platform, high above a series of sculptured steps. Below the platform covered in darkness was a ledge in the shape of a cone, giving Jimmy the impression of an ice-cream. Again, there was nothing supporting the platform or steps. They were just hanging.

Jimmy saw something sparkling on the top of the platform, almost glowing and radiating light in hundreds of different directions.

The pair picked up the pace to a gentle jog and quickly reached the steps. They climbed them one by one; soon the platform was within touching distance and Jimmy took a final step. Instantly small dust fragments fell into the void below, then, without warning the path completely crumbled and disintegrated below their feet as though it had been made from wet sand.

There was nothing the pair could do, the path had gone. As they fell they both managed to take hold of the edge of the jagged top step, which was still attached to the platform, floating unsupported in the air. The pair were holding on to the step with their bare fingertips and they could both feel droplets of blood trickle down their hands from the razor sharp edges.

They frantically scrambled with their feet and managed to find some footholds in the cone shaped rock face hanging underneath the platform, which gave them greater stability. The pair remained there, dangling, trying not to look down when Jimmy started to try and console Talula, telling her things would be okay; they had survived worse.

The deep grisly voice rasped again, "Congratulations on getting this far, you have both done well; for that I will try and help you."

The light tinkling sound of glass delicately rolling along the saucer shaped platform above them echoed though the empty blackness as though blown by an invisible breath.

The voice breathed deeply.

"Jimmy, on the ledge just above your right hand is a necklace with a green emerald stone. If you grab this you will then need to make a decision. This stone will help you with the predicament you are in but it can only save one of you. Choose carefully!"

The sinister voice disappeared as Jimmy was reminded of the burning sensation of the sore cuts on his hands. Scrabbling around in a panic Jimmy reached up with his right hand and felt around. As he patted he felt the stone but hit it further out of his reach as he fumbled. He took a deep breath and gave a last big effort and then he grabbed it! It was in his hand and he was ready to get out of this situation.

He held the stone for a few moments and it started to glow brighter and brighter. The stone mesmerized Jimmy, but he remembered what the voice had said; "This stone will help you with the predicament you are in, but it can only save one of you."

He looked across at Talula. He saw her in a different light. She was vulnerable, scared, but he wasn't. He knew what he had signed up for, he couldn't live with himself if he survived this, but had to carry on with the knowledge that he lived but could have saved someone else.

Jimmy's grip was getting weaker as he managed to swap the emerald stone into his left hand before reaching out and handing it to Talula. As he passed the stone he knew this decision was the end for him.

Talula looked into Jimmy's eyes; she could see what the gesture meant and she could see he was sacrificing himself, but she knew she was weak. Talula knew this couldn't be the end for her and slowly reached out with her right hand and grasped the stone with all her life.

She gave a solemn smile as a tear gently cascaded down her cheeks and she whispered the words "Thank you," smiling in appreciation.

The green emerald stone provided a magnitude of pure light as soon as Talula placed it around her neck. Within an instant the ground that Jimmy had been gripping onto and resting his feet in crumbled and he slid down into the darkness without a sound.

Jimmy had made peace with himself, he was ready. He looked back up at Talula as he fell, having no idea what fate had in store for him.

Closing his eyes, gravity forced him down.

To his amazement and against all the rules of physics he started to slow in mid fall and after only a few seconds landed on his feet a few metres below. Surprised, he looked up at Talula and saw that she was wearing the glowing stone but was locked in suspended animation.

Jimmy shouted up to her, but there was no reply, no movement and no acknowledgement. As he gathered his bearings he looked forward and saw a path leading into a passage. Taking a deep breath and summoning yet more courage he walked through the doorway.

He saw a grand room decorated with expensive ornaments, artwork and gold goblets. It was a room befitting a king.

The room was lit by a series of hovering green and yellow flames suspended high above in the air. In front of Jimmy were ten or more black stone steps leading down to a roaring yellow fire, billowing out of a stone circular pit filled with a bright red fluid.

The thing that Jimmy wanted the most was waiting in this room … answers.

Standing in front of the spectacular fire was a short, golden haired old man, crouched over and holding a wooden stick. His shoulder length golden hair rested gently down the spine of his back and a long golden beard hung down the front, neatly tied in place.

The elderly man's face was severely wrinkled, and his eyebrows were far too bushy, much bushier than any Jimmy had ever seen before. The little old man wore a fine yellow silk robe that covered his knees, with tight blue trousers and red slippers. In his left hand he held a wooden walking cane. Jimmy glanced at the stick and noticed that the handle was in the shape of a grand owl.

The old man struggled, eventually lifting his head up to look at Jimmy. As their eyes met the old man slowly raised his right hand in a claw position and Jimmy felt a tug from the inside of his jacket. Before Jimmy had time to react the Blood Map flittered upwards into the air, folded itself into the shape of a paper bird and gently flapped its wings, gliding into the strange man's right hand.

"Haha, I didn't summon the Blood Map—it remembers its last master and goes to those it is attuned to. It would be drawn to you if I now left!"

Jimmy was unsure what that meant, but knew instantly that this was the voice, the voice that had been speaking to him and his companions throughout their journey in this mountain.

"Who are you? What happened to Talula?" demanded Jimmy.

"Have no fear about Talula, or for that matter, your other friends, they are safe and unharmed. You don't think the Elders would have created a sanctuary like this and sent you on a deadly quest knowing that you all may perish."

The old man turned and looked beyond the flame, clapping his hands.

Brilliant sky blue lights appeared from the ceiling and projected solid beams down next to the fire. As the bright light faded Jimmy could gradually see that his friends had been transported within the beams and that they were safe and well, but still locked in suspended animation.

"I knew it would be you Jimmy, you would be the one who was pure of heart, the one to defeat the challenges. I have been watching you for many years. The last challenge was particularly difficult. You had the power to save yourself in the palm of your hand but you selflessly gave it to another.

"You would both have come into this sanctuary if Talula had not accepted the emerald. But, as she willingly allowed your fate, then she is not pure of heart."

Jimmy asked his question again, but this time with more venom,

"Who are you?"

The old man smiled, looked Jimmy in the eye and rolled up his right sleeve. On his right forearm Jimmy saw it, a number *6* burnt into his skin.

"I, Jimmy, am Argon Monteith."

Jimmy gasped; "But we read Lady Aurabella's diary, you created a trap to defeat Tyranacus! He destroyed you and the others disappeared!"

Argon smiled. "It certainly was a long time ago; arh Aurabella, she became a good friend to me, but she wouldn't join my army of Light Dwellers. I tried and tried to convince her, but she kept telling me not to be foolish.

"It was a treacherous night, many, many years after we found the Amulet of Trident. We grew even more powerful, but from the start I knew what we were doing wasn't right, I didn't want to destroy this world. I have watched you Jimmy, I know you feel the same way now?"

"No," said Jimmy gritting his teeth. "I need the power, I will become all powerful, release Tyranacus and together we will destroy the Gatekeeper!"

"Don't be foolish Jimmy, that's not how this works; you have been done a great wrong. Your father wasn't killed by the Gatekeeper, it was someone even closer to your heart. Lyreco is feeding you lies to make you help them. That is what they do, that's how they manipulate you to do their bidding.

"But that is why I am here. I knew it would be you who succeeded in the challenges, as I did two millennia ago. Jimmy, we are one and the same, the Blood Map will only come to those of a certain bloodline … ours. I was more powerful than my companions and you are far more so than yours. The reason is because there is good pulsing through your blood, and Lyreco needed to destroy that somehow. They learnt from the mistakes with me and had to find a way to force out the good within you and ensure you helped them.

"Two millennia ago I became fearful with the quests that we were being sent on. We were asked to destroy homes, collect wealth and destroy anyone in our paths. I loved that world, the people, my family, and the thought of Tyranacus destroying it made me crazy.

"After a few years, I used the power and the training I had received to train others, people with special gifts, but for good. The Light Dwellers were three brave warriors and we devised a trap. We would summon the mighty demon and whilst my companions were distracted and unsuspecting they would be neutralized; our combined powers would be used to destroy the raging beast.

"The plan failed, he was far too powerful, more powerful than we had ever expected. He attacked the Light Dwellers, injuring two of them; they were lying burnt on the floor.

"When I sent a series of attacks to stop him he turned and with his humongous beast-like frame charged at me at great speed. I tried to turn and run but he was on me in a flash. I fired everything I had at him, but he deflected it away and struck me across the chest with the mighty axe.

"I was sent soaring, crashing off the edge of the canyon. I grabbed onto the edge with the ends of my fingers but I knew it was over, the Light Dwellers and I were defeated and the world was finished. My fingers gave in and I fell to what everyone believed was my end.

"I fell a great way towards the jagged, razor sharp rocks below, but just as I was covered by the sea mist I morphed into my inner power and drifted away, crashing into the water. I awoke in a solitary cave some days later and remained there, in fear of my life as I heard the cries of the world around me being destroyed.

"We planned the attack that day, but we didn't anticipate how powerful the beast was. This was the second plan ... to wait for you. I knew you would arise from my bloodline. I knew you would pass the challenges alone, and I have survived all these years, to pass the message that you don't need to do this. We can help you.

"You will need to continue your training to become more powerful, but you must destroy your friends before Tyranacus is released, it is the only way."

Jimmy stepped back. "Why should I believe you; why should I help you?"

"Jimmy, you know that what I speak is the truth. I know you agree that what they want you to do is wrong, but you have a choice. The Amulet you seek is in the flame, take it, and never let it be known we have spoken. Think about what I have said, Jimmy. I will always be watching you, all you have to do is summon me and we will talk again."

With that Argon morphed into a yellow-eyed owl, the one that had been following him since he could remember, and flew off upward through a small hole in the cave ceiling.

Jimmy found it difficult to take in what he had been told. Emotions were flooding through him. Had he been tricked? What did he mean, the 'Gatekeeper hadn't killed his father'? What did he mean, it was 'someone close to him'? Who? *How do I know Argon isn't tricking me now? Why did Aurabella write that he had been destroyed?*

Jimmy's thoughts were broken by the roaring flame before him at the bottom of the steps. He walked down the solid black steps and started to circle the mysterious flame. He couldn't work out how to get the Amulet out of the small inferno. Jimmy slowly put his hand close to the fire, ready to withdraw it as soon as the burning sensation started. To Jimmy's surprise the flame started to bend around his hand.

The flame reminded him of the one he had plunged his hands into the night he first received his inner creature. With the fear now drained away, and the desire to complete the quest, he once again plunged both hands into the fire.

His hands caught up with the retracting flame, which caused a chain reaction and his whole body illuminated bright green, the same colour as his inner power.

Seconds later both flames dampened down and an awe inspiring, beautiful, perfectly formed diamond shaped stone lifted into the air. The glowing stone was hovering and he couldn't take his eyes off of it. It was perfectly cut and glistening.

Looking closely, he saw that a thin layer of gold separated the diamond into four different coloured stones.

Jimmy was transfixed by the jewel and grabbed out with his right hand, clutching it and bringing it closer. However the second Jimmy touched the stone it imploded, sending rays of pure light streaming throughout the room. The light was blinding and all Jimmy could do was shield his eyes.

The stone split into four segments, hovered, then spun before shooting through the air like shrapnel, hitting the three suspended youths in the chest. The piece intended for Jimmy also hit him square in the chest, knocking the breath out of him. He tried to move but he too was now suspended on the spot. The last thing Jimmy remembered was seeing the arms of his companions splayed out like a star; a beam projected upward from the stone and their eyes began to glow blue. The power channelled up into the sky.

Chapter 25

The lone owl flapped its wings as it soared through the night sky.

The owl eventually found the building it had been looking for and circled the unassuming public museum. Noticing that the passage was clear it slowly and gently swooped down and as it landed on the multitude of steps leading to the entrance the owl morphed into a golden haired old man and collapsed on the top step.

The old man rested for a few moments to regain his strength, and looking up, he could see the secure entrance doors. With the last of his strength he pulled himself to his feet and staggered to the door. The old man concentrated, sending a surge of power through his right hand which magnetized the electronic doors, causing their locks to release.

Staggering through the entrance, using his stick as support, he walked through the metal detector. The alarm sounded, echoing throughout the empty building.

Argon pushed through to the ancient Egyptian exhibit, panting and wheezing from exhaustion. There he plodded to four ancient, faded capsules that looked to be from a time even before the Egyptian period. One of the capsules was open, but the other three were securely fastened. The three capsules had a series of dents and indentations where archaeologists had spent centuries trying to force them open, to no avail.

The old man approached the strange stone capsules, pulled the wooden owl head off his cane and threw it into the air.

The owl revolved with the pull of gravity and released a trail of golden dust flakes. The wooden owl hit the floor, bounced three times, and as though drawn by a vacuum the flakes flew into the locks of the three capsules.

The capsules reacted and a surge of light went through the seams as the solid stone doors opened, grinding the floor as they did. This act took the last of Argon's strength and he collapsed to the floor; the last thing he heard was the thud of loud boots walking all around him.

Moments passed and Argon started to come around; with blurred vision he saw an image he had forgotten existed. He thought he was still dreaming, but then the sweet smell of perfume hit him like an anvil. The sweet smelling vision helped the old man up and then she spoke with the voice of an angel.

"Argon, you did it, I can't believe it, you kept your promise, you kept us safe, you held on, after all of this time!"

The young lady helped the old man to a wooden seat next to the capsules. The smell sent Argon's senses tingling, but the voice took him back to a time he couldn't even remember. Slowly his eyes began to focus, and there she was; a vision of pure beauty. Argon was shocked that she looked exactly the same as she did the last day he had seen her, not knowing if he would live long enough to see this day.

The old man tried to speak, but started slurring his words through exhaustion. All he could do was look at her radiant face.

"Don't try to speak, Argon, you are very weak, you need to rest, we will help you!" said the tall slim female with light brown hair.

Her eyes glowed hazel and her smile illuminated the room. As Argon glanced down he saw she was still wearing her black cloak with the bright red lining. Argon leant back, closing his eyes to rest.

The emotion brought back memories from a time long ago. The four young adults were standing in the Elksidian Forest, where they had freed their minds and using their array of powers summoned the mighty Tyranacus. Instantly Argon sprang the trap. Argon turned to his unsuspecting and defenceless companions and fired a single bolt of lightning at close range, which sent the three young adults through the air, landing unconscious in the distance.

It was Aurabella who had the hardest impact, landing backwards into a tree and hitting her head. Argon looked and a veil of guilt flooded over him, but he couldn't help, he knew the plan, it was the only plan. Higuain, the brown haired vision, was first to drop from the tree and sent a series of attacks at the vulnerable and still forming Tyranacus. Argon also sent a number of lightning bolts hitting the emerging beast in the head, chest and legs. Between the pair of them they managed to force the creature onto his knees.

Stratos came charging out of the woodland like a man with fury. He was a giant of a man, with long unkempt, wild red hair, a long beard, wearing fur armour and carrying an axe nearly the same size as the demon's. Stratos charged and struck a mighty blow downward toward the beast. The beast raised its axe and the pair collided, echoing the sound of thunder throughout the wood.

Stratos couldn't form an inner power or send any form of projectile. His power surged from his arms into his weapon, which was unstoppable. The third Light Dweller was Dravid. He was a water healer, he could evaporate when near water, become one with it and then use its power to heal the injured or weary.

Dravid was a pacifist; he had no power of offence; he did however agree to help the Light Dwellers defeat the immortal demon for the good of the earth.

Dravid stood back from the fight, watching intently in case one of his companions needed his help. As he watched the mighty duel between Tyranacus and Stratos he became aware of the helpless female, mortally injured and lying on the tree.

Dravid knew the mission and knew the purpose, but he couldn't leave her like this. He quickly ran past the onslaught and grabbed Aurabella's head. As he did he could feel the cut as the blood seeped through his fingers, dripping to the floor. Looking around he saw that her companions were also still unconscious, but uninjured.

As Dravid's arms caressed the back of Aurabella's head his right hand started to lose its definition and turned to gel, then water. He closed his eyes as they were submerged in a sea of pure light blue. Seconds passed and Aurabella gasped a deep breath. Dravid turned her on her side and returned to his companions.

The clatter of heavy metal continued to rasp through the air as sparks flew every time the pair clashed. Stratos struck a mighty blow at Tyranacus and the beast responded, blocking the strike with both hands on its axe. Seeing their chance that the creature was vulnerable and distracted both Argon and Higuain sent a series of attacks at the beast, hitting him square on the back.

The creature staggered, stumbled, then dropped to one knee. The battle was over; the Light Dwellers had won against all odds. Tyranacus was defenceless. Stratos raised his mighty axe to administer the final blow. The axe was above his head and with all the fury, all the aggression he had, he struck downward.

Then, from the other side of the battle field, came a flash of light that would change the world forever.

Aurabella had gained enough composure and sent a ball of fire, hitting Stratos in the back and sending his axe crashing to the ground. Stratos hit the floor and his cloak lit in purple and black flames.

"Nooo!! What have I done?" screamed Dravid.

The demon stood up, looking down at the burnt warrior who until moments ago had won the battle. Stratos was severely injured and posed no threat to Tyranacus.

The creature turned and charged at Argon, swinging his axe in fury. The pair clashed as Argon sent wave after wave of attack, but the demon parried them. Argon was being forced to the edge of the cliff by the sheer power of the beast and as he turned to give one last longing look at Higuain, the demon struck him across the chest with his glistening axe, sending the chosen one toppling over the edge of the cliff.

Argon's earlier memories had betrayed him. It had been too long ago but the memories now came flooding back. Days after the heavy battle, he was dragged from the deathly waters by the remorseful Dravid. The healer in his water form searched for days to locate the hero and finally grabbed him before the sea dragged him under.

The still weary Argon was pulled to a nearby cave away from the Armageddon. Dravid explained that after the heavy defeat he and Higuain managed to escape, taking Stratos with them. He explained that Stratos was mortally injured but he had managed to heal him.

The group knew it was the end so they reverted to the backup plan devised by Argon. If the plan failed they would return to their sanctuary and seal themselves into an eclipse portal, a stone capsule that would send them to a state of hibernation until they were released.

Argon was lying face down in the sand, and Dravid pulled at his sleeve.

"Come on, we need to go, we must get to safety before the purge."

Argon smiled and looked at his friend.

"There is no escape Dravid, there couldn't be a Plan B for all of us. Someone has to stay outside, survive this atrocity somehow. Once you are sealed, only I can open it and release you all.

"Dravid, you must return: leave me here, tell Higuain I love her and seal yourselves in. When the time is right, when the next rising is foretold, I will release you on the new world."

"Don't be foolish, Argon, how will you survive?"

"Please Dravid, time is of the essence, you must go. Go back before it is too late. I will find you and one day you will be released!"

And there it was decided. The lonely warrior would walk the earth unaccompanied, amidst the chaos and evil that followed. All Argon could do was hide until the time was right.

Chapter 26

Jimmy had no control over his body. His arms and legs were being pulled out into the shape of a star and he was being sucked high towards the middle of the room along with his companions.

He could feel the pressure on his chest and body, but he was physically frozen in place by this mysterious blue beam. The group were suspended in the air for a few moments when Jimmy felt a severe burning sensation in his chest, as though someone was pulling his heart from his body.

Managing to divert his eyes down he saw the segment of the Amulet of Trident being ripped from his chest by an invisible hand; it drifted along with the three other pieces.

The fragmented amulet hovered for a few seconds and then, as if summoned by a powerful magnet, the pieces flew toward each other in a haze of bright light and reunited to recreate the original, perfect diamond shape.

There was a second flash of light and the Amulet of Trident started to violently shake and rumble. As the group helplessly looked on, a bright sea green beam projected high into the ceiling.

Within the beam the image of a huge, gaunt face appeared.

The face was ancient, wrinkled and frightening. Although the image projected was sea green, brown wild hair fluttered in the air steams as the image flickered. The image's unkempt moustache hung clawing onto the withering upper lip and extended past its chin.

As the group looked on, powerless, the image's eyes sharply opened, revealing tiny, pure black eyes which had seen centuries of destruction and death.

There was a minute's pause and in a deep voice that sent an echo trembling throughout the grand room, the image spoke,

"WHO DARES WAKE LORD TRIDENT?"

The group could not have spoken if they wanted too, but the Elder was so powerful he didn't need a verbal response. The image gritted its teeth, which instantly and violently forced the heads of the four children back as their eyes glazed over pure white.

The Elder looked into all of their eyes at once and saw their lives flash instantly before him. Then, the sleeve on each of the group's right arms slowly dissolved into nothing, showing the bare skin on their forearms. The image blinked its eyes and the four 6's illuminated the colour of demonic red, instantly channelling upwards through their blood, along their jaw lines and into their eyes, snapping them from pure white to blood red.

"Good, my children, you have done well to successfully pass this test, good. I have looked through your eyes at your past and I have seen your future. I have foreseen that you will raise the indestructible beast Tyranacus and this world will be laid to rub …"

With that last word the image of Trident flinched and riled back as if in severe pain.

"It can't be!" roared the image in fury.

"The beast is awoken, but a flash of bright light masked the end. I have never seen this before, what to make of it all? Nevertheless, once the beast is awoken, there is no stopping it. I will reflect on this image.

"In the meantime, I have felt each of your powers. You all bear the mark of Tyranacus and will one day lead him into battle to destroy this pathetic world. However, there is so much more to learn, so many new powers to possess. I have input my power and will within Lyreco.

"He is but a simple man I found many years ago, a lost soul, but I gave him a purpose and implanted the way you four should learn and be trained. I can see that one of you intends to battle the keeper of life and death himself.

"Hahaha. If that is your wish: but this petty issue is no concern of mine. First you will do my bidding and purge this world. The Amulet will be returned to you and with it you will be able to break the Elders' seal and gain access to the ancient mysteries of Sepura Castle.

"Be warned, just because you have access, does not mean you will have free rein. Certain parts of the building will only be opened on your advancement, but by checking your memories, I see you fulfilled your first quest and a new surprise gift will be bestowed upon you!"

On his last word the Amulet of Trident fragmented again, gently hovered, humming, to the chests of the four warriors, and slotted back into place.

"My children," the echoing voice rasped again. "Take heed of my warnings, and you will be the most powerful warriors ever to walk this earth."

The four children, still hanging in animation, watched as the last remnants of Lord Trident's image flickered away and in a heartbeat the projected beam suspending the four of them disappeared and the group started to fall the great distance to the hard ground.

Jimmy could feel the pressure and could see the hard ground coming closer and closer. He, along with the others, closed his eyes and braced for impact, when the world seemed to go quiet. They had stopped in mid fall as a fresh gentle breeze flowed past their faces.

Jimmy dared not open his eyes but apprehensively lowered his feet and surprisingly felt a carpet of luscious grass below them. Opening his eyes he found he was hovering just above the ground but once his body registered that he could touch the floor; gravity took over and he landed on the ground with a thud.

The others also landed, but quickly got up and ran to each other giving a considerable embrace. Only a few hours ago Jimmy had thought he had seen the last of his companions. Jimmy saved the biggest hug for Talula and whispered to her, "I'm glad you are okay."

The sharp realisation that they were all safe and well meant that they hadn't even noticed the awe-inspiring castle overshadowing them.

The group turned and looked up at Sepura Castle in great surprise. Standing on a large grass bank, a gravel path led to a solid wooden bridge over a violent, flowing black river.

Beyond the bridge was an enormous, thick wooden castle drawbridge with two coats of armour, positioned either side.

In the middle of the drawbridge was a diamond-shaped indentation. *That must be where the Amulet of Trident is positioned*, thought Jimmy. They approached cautiously and started to cross the bridge, peering over the wooden railing into the black sea.

To the group's surprise the black substance wasn't water or anything close. When they looked closer they could see the outline of white images floating within the blackness. As the group looked, one of the white spirits glared upward and sprang up from the 'water', causing the group to step back.

The white creature landed back into the water and harmlessly drifted off back upstream. The motion of stepping back also made the group aware of people watching them.

Turning, they saw in the near distance Lyreco and Xanadu standing, holding the majestic white unicorns, looking radiant in the morning sun as the wind gently ruffled their white feathers and the sun sparkled off their horns.

The group approached the grand wooden drawbridge standing directly in front of the diamond shape. Instantly they felt the burning sensation in their chests and the fragments lurched away from them and drifted, reforming as they approached the indentation.

The diamond shape locked into place and the gaps filled with a golden seal. Instantly the diamond started to glow blood red and four beams shot from the centre of the diamond, streamed past the group and hit the four unsuspecting unicorns on the top of their horns.

The horses started to shudder and in front of the group their skin colour became darker and darker until they were standing as black as night. The mighty beasts all rose on their rear legs and began to violently kick the air.

Within seconds they landed on the ground and were an awe-inspiring sight. The flowing white unicorns now stood pure black. Their eyes were now an intense fiery red and they were all blowing aggressive condensation from their noses. This gave the impression of smoke being released from the fire within their souls.

As the group stared at their new prized possessions the horses reacted and each started dragging their hooves violently on the dusty ground. The feathers fell off the creatures' wings one by one and the wings themselves morphed with sharper more fearsome features and presented the image that they were wings of a vampire bat, but large enough to tear the roof from a house.

The horses snorted fiery smoke once more, violently snapping away from Xanadu and Lyreco, who had been holding them with rope, and soared high into the sky leaving a thrust of air in their wake and causing Xanadu to stagger backwards.

With their new venomous beasts gliding through the air, Harry returned to the door to await its grand opening. The beams stopped firing at the unicorns and there was a brief pause as the anticipation started to rise within the group.

The stone started to rumble and shake. This time though, with a flash of four red lights, the beams hit the unsuspecting children in the centre of their heads. The surge of immense power caused the children's mark of Tyranacus to glow bright red, but it also caused the group to fall to their knees.

Their 6's were glowing red-hot, illuminating the bridge. As the group felt the surge of power coursing through their veins they looked upward and saw that the wooden drawbridge was starting to creak slowly open and they knew that the immense power, which lay ahead, would soon be theirs.

Jimmy gave a maniacal smile, knowing that this was the first step to receiving the power to enact his ultimate revenge and destroy the Gatekeeper for what he had done to his father.

The adventure continues in:

Jimmy Threepwood and the Elixir of Light

Thank you for taking the time to read this book. If you liked it, please consider telling your friends or posting a short review on Goodreads or the site where you bought it. Word of mouth is an author's best friend and much appreciated.

About the Author

Rich Pitman was born in Newport, South Wales. He now lives in the picturesque Forest of Dean which is situated in the western part of the county of Gloucestershire, England.

Rich is the author of the popular children's series following the life of a young boy, Jimmy Threepwood, who is one day destined to destroy the world. The first book in the five-book series is Jimmy Threepwood and the Veil of Darkness, which was voted as a finalist for the People's Book Prize.

People's Book Prize Finalist - Jimmy Threepwood and the Veil of Darkness:
http://www.peoplesbookprize.com/section.php?id=7
https://www.facebook.com/jimmy.threepwood
Wordpress: http://jimmythreepwoodblog.wordpress.com/
Pinterest: https://pinterest.com/jimmythreepwood/
Twitter - @threepwoodbooks
https://www.goodreads.com/author/show/6439938.Rich_
Pitman
https://www.linkedin.com/in/rich-pitman-3427bb5b

Lightning Source UK Ltd.
Milton Keynes UK
UKHW021633251118
332960UK00006B/85/P

9 781681 604268